BUDDHA'S CRYSTAL

BUDDHA'S CRYSTAL

AND

OTHER FAIRY STORIES

BY

YEI THEODORA OZAKI

Author of "Japanese Fairy Tales"

RNU PRESS

BARRIE, CANADA

——

2010

Ozaki, Yei Thodora : Japanese Fairy Tales

This Edition Originally Published :
    Tokyo : Kelly & Walsh : 1908

This Edition :
    Barrie : RNU Press : 2010

Re-Typset in : Adobe Caslon Pro ®

Republished by: David Edwards (RNU Press)
555 Mapleview Drive West
Barrie, ON, L4N 8W2
www.rnupress.com

RNU PRESS

ISBN: 978-0-9812886-4-2

PREFACE

THE kind reception given to " The Japanese Fairy Book" both in the West and in the East has encouraged me to send forth another small collection of stories from Japan. I have invented none of these stories. They are taken from Mr. Hideo Iwaya's modern version of the old-folk-lore tales of Japan and some of his new stories, and in clothing them with an English dress my work has been that of adapter rather than translator. In picturesqueness of conception Japanese stories yield the palm to none. And they are rich in quaint expressions and dainty conceits. But they are apt to be written in a style too bold. This defect the professional story-teller remedies by colouring his story as he tells it. In the same way I have tried to brighten the rather bare structure of a story, where it seemed to need such treatment, with touches of local colour so as to make the story more attractive to the foreign reader. Whether I have succeeded or not the reader must judge for himself.

"Buddha's Crystal" first appeared in the *Lady's Realm* and is here reprinted by the kind consent of the publishers as is also "The Tea Kettle of Good Fortune " and "The Mouse Bride" which first appeared in the *Girl's Realm* in 1899 when that magazine belonged to the same firm.* My thanks are also due to the present owners† of the *Girl's Realm* for allowing me to add " Issunboshi " (1900) to this collection.

"The Demon Tile" and "The Fallen Comet" are re-written from a translation given me by a friend who permitted me to make what use I liked of them. These two stories and the " Crysanthemum Crest" are, I believe, newly invented by Mr. Iwaya.

The illustrations have been drawn by Mr. Tosen Toda and Mr. Shusui Okakura. To both of whom grateful acknowledgement is due for painstaking collaboration.

Tokyo, 1908.

Y. T. O.

* Hutchinson & Co.   † Cassell & Co.

Buddha's Crystal

L ONG, long ago there lived in Japan a great State Minister named Kamatari Ko. He was descended from the illustrious Fujiwara Uji, and was the ancestor of the five great noble families from whose circle only the brides of the Emperors could be chosen. Kamatari was known throughout the land, not only as a knight of the most noble descent, but also as a wise and able minister and a loyal and faithful subject, devoted to his master, the Emperor, Tenshii Tenno, to whom he had rendered signal service in quelling the insurrection raised by the rebel Soga-no-Iruka, and in restoring peace and unity to the land.

Now Kamatari, besides being rich and prosperous and of illustrious fame, was thrice happy in the possession of one beautiful daughter, named Kohaku Jo. She was the light of his eye, the joy of his heart, and the pride of his life, and he vowed, each time he saw her growing in youthful loveliness, like a peach-blossom in the sunshine of spring, that none but a king should be her mate. But of his ambition he spoke to none, and people wondered why, when one after another of the noble youths were offered by their families according to Eastern custom, as suitors to her hand, ceremoniously worded excuses were made to all ; but so it was.

And Kohaku Jo grew in grace and beauty as the years went by, and at sixteen years of age all who saw her said that she was the most beautiful princess they had ever seen. Though small, she was as slender as a lily-stalk ; her face was a small oval, delicately pale, with cheeks of the soft cherry bloom, and her eyebrows like the outline of the crescent moon. Fair indeed was she to behold. Her mouth was like a tiny bud of the peach-blossom, and her hands and feet rivalled the snowy petals of the white lotus.

But far outshining her loveliness of form was her loveliness of character and disposition, and far more precious, too, in the sight of all her friends. Never had she been known to speak a harsh word to anyone or to disobey her parents in her whole life. Except to go at appointed festivals and family anniversaries to the great temple hard by, whose massive roof she could see daily looming through the great pine and cryptomeria trees of her home, she never left the precincts of the palace. At such times she might be seen arranging flowers and pouring water over the monumental gravestones of the family, or in the beautiful solemn temple itself burning incense before the tablets set up to the memory of her ancestors, or clapping her hands and bowing her dusky head before the holy shrine.

Her days thus passed quietly and peacefully in the unbroken seclusion and retirement of an Eastern princess, and little recked she of the future that her father dreamed of her. But her fate was drawing near, though she knew it not. Kamatari was certainly favoured of the gods. His ambitious hopes for his daughter were soon to be realised.

One day there was a great stir in the palace courtyard, and the officers of ceremony were rushing to and fro to find out what was the reason of the unusual commotion there. The big gates were thrown open, and in came a stately procession of men carrying a banner with the strange device of a dragon on a yellow background. They were envoys from the Court of China, and they came with a message from the Emperor Koso. He had heard of the beauty, the grace, and the wit of Kohaku Jo, and he sent to offer her his hand and the half of his kingdom. Should her father consent to give her to the Emperor of China, Kohaku Jo might choose out of the vast treasures of her adopted country to enrich the land of her birth and its temples.

The envoys were received with great pomp and ceremony, a whole wing of the palace was placed at their disposal, and Kamatari begged them to give him a few days in which to consider the matter. He would give them a final answer when he had spoken with his daughter. She was but a little maid still, and she must be told without undue haste. With many prostrations on both sides, Kamatari, the gratified father, withdrew. But in his heart there was no hesitation though much ceremony.

On reaching his own room he clapped his hands, and when in answer to his summons his confidential servant appeared, he sent him to bid the Lady Kohaku Jo hie to her father's presence. The messenger found her seated before the *koto* (harp) with her attendants around her, and when told that her father called for her, she hastened to obey, wondering what made him wish to see her so suddenly.

She reached her father's room, and, pushing aside the sliding screens, she slipped inside on to the creamy white mats, and bowed to the ground before him.

" Honourable father, you sent for me ; I am here ! "

"Yes, Kohaku, I sent for you to tell you a great piece of news. The time has come for you to leave your father's home. You must marry now. As your mother and I have often told you, you must marry some day, someone whom we should deem a fitting husband for you. This day have I chosen for you, my daughter. The Emperor of China has sent for you to become his bride, and in six weeks you must depart with the ambassadors who will conduct you to your future home."

" Honourable father, must I leave you and my mother so soon? " and the maiden's face grew pale and her eyes filled with tears ; " and must I go away across the seas to a land which I have never seen ? Is this your wish ? "

"Yes, Kohaku, my daughter, such is my wish. All women must marry sooner or later, it is their duty, and in your new home you will soon be happy—happier than you have ever been before. You will be a Queen, and the Emperor places all the riches and the treasures of his kingdom at your feet. Think what you will be able to do for your beloved Temple of Kofukuji, where you were carried to be blessed when but a babe of one hundred days old. Come, my daughter, do not look so grave and sad ! Are you not happy at the thought of the splendid prospect before you ? Have I not chosen well for you ? "

Kohaku had been brought up to consider her father's will as law, and she never even thought of doing anything but obeying him. So she clasped her tiny white hands together on the matted floor, and bowing over them said :

"I obey you, my father, now as always. I am only sad at the idea of leaving my home and my mother and going so very far away ; but since it is your wish it must be good for me."

So little Kohaku calmly accepted her fate, and went back to her companions to tell them of what should happen. When they heard the news they hid their pretty faces in their long sleeves, and wept with grief at the thought of parting with Kohaku, who also wept in sympathy.

While they were thus sorrowfully sitting together, Kohaku's mother came into the room, and told them to dry their tears, for some of them were to be chosen to go with Kohaku, and fitting arrangements would be made for their return to Japan after the marriage. Then they smiled again, and one or two of the little ladies-in-waiting leant forward and stroked their young mistress's hand, and vowed that they would stay with her always, even in China, for their love for her was as high as the mountains and as deep as the sea.

Thus it was that the beautiful daughter of Kamatari Ko sailed away across the seas to China and became the bride of the Chinese Emperor.

But before she went she made a pilgrimage to the great Temple Kofukuji. She had grown up almost under the shadow of the great sloping roof, and the sound ot the deep-toned bell rolling out its voluminous note on the still air at the hours of sunrise and sunset had marked her day's-rising and night's resting as long as ever she could remember. So when the wonder and the fear of the unknown swelled her young heart to restlessness and to the first questionings of fate and of the future, she arose, and calling her favourite nurse, told her to follow her to the temple, for she was going to pray. At night she went, walking barefoot to the shrine through the snow, for it was winter, to ask for protection, and she vowed that if it were granted to her to arrive safely in the strange land to which she was being sent as a bride, she would search for three inestimable treasures, which she would send to the temple as a thank-offering.

II.

AND Kohaku's prayer was heard. Her journey was accomplished in all safety, and she was married with great magnificence to the Emperor Koso of China. And at last she stood before the Emperor, her bridegroom, after the long ceremony and the many Court festivities were over. She had great courage and pride, but she could not help trembling a little, for her heart was more full of doubt and fear than of hope and joy.

"What would this new husband be like?" she asked herself. "Would her father's last comforting words come true—that she should be happy, and that in the Emperor's love and care she should find more than all she had left behind—country, parents, home, and friends? And how, above all, was she to know what were the duties of the wife of an Emperor? Would it be in her power to please this great man? If only she might return to her father and mother again—to her old quiet life——"

Before she could think again the Emperor was by her side. He took her hand in his, raising it to his cheek and forehead in tender deference, while his voice sounded low and sweet in her ear. Fear fled now, and she found courage to look up into his face for the first time, and then

she saw that his dark eyes rested on her kindly and loving-
ly, as he said :

" Little cherry flower of Japan, they lied not when they
told me that you were beautiful. The artist did not paint
your portrait half fair enough. Do not fear, for I love you
and will make you happy. After long, long days of weary
waiting, I have gathered the '*azalea of the distant mountain*,'
and now I plant it in my garden, and great is the gladness
of my heart ! "

The Emperor fulfilled his promise as an Emperor
should. Happy indeed was Kohaku. Sudden summer
seemed to kindle all her ways, and her life thrilled to the
new joy of her husband's love. He led her from palace to
palace, and showed her all the wonders of his kingdom and
the splendour of his houses.

At last they came to one in the summertime, cool and
shady and restful in the shadow of the green hills, and
being weary of much travelling and sight-seeing she begged the Emperor to let her stay there for a little while.
Hand in hand they wandered through the spacious halls
and under the long avenues of lofty trees, or were rowed
out in the cool of the evenings on the lake, from whence
they glanced back at the illuminated palace and thousands
of coloured lanterns which festooned the gardens, rivalling
in brilliancy the starlit heavens over their heads.

As the breath of spring warms the chill earth, barren
so long in the cold clutch of winter, to a sudden burst of

wealth and beauty, so happiness sometimes transforms the faces and forms of those to whom it comes. Kohaku grew more beautiful, unfolding like a rosebud to maturer loveliness in the warmth of the sunshine of love, and the Emperor said to himself that he would cause her name and her beauty to be remembered for ever.

So he called together his goldsmiths and gardeners, and commanded them to fashion a path for the Empress such as had never before been heard ot in the wide world. The stepping-stones of this path were to be lotus-flowers, carved out of silver and gold, for her to walk on whenever she strolled forth under the trees or by the lake, so that it might be said that her beautiful feet were never soiled by touching the earth ; and ever since then, in China and in Japan, poet-lovers and lover-poets in song and sonnet and sweet conversation have called the feet of the women they loved " lotus-feet."

But for all the great change from the simple maiden life to the regal splendour which surrounded her as wife of the Chinese Emperor, Kohaku forgot not the land of her birth, nor the vow which she had vowed in the Temple of Kofukuji, and in the happy days spent in the Palace of the Lotus Path she found confidence to tell her husband with what great timidity she had ventured on her new life, and of her intention to send thank-offerings to the temple in Japan in grateful recognition of answered prayer and the happiness she had found in married life.

"Help me, august lord, to choose something that is worthy of the chosen wife of your Majesty, and let its value be in proportion to the degree of my prosperity, which is great beyond all words."

The Emperor was pleased at her request. He ordered his treasure-houses to be opened and the best of their contents to be brought to him. Day after day the happy Emperor and his bride sat together looking at the quantities of wonderful things that were laid at their feet, surprised at the immensity of their own possessions. To Kohaku it seemed as if she had been transported to fairyland, so many and varied were the treasures that were brought to the palace daily. Each store-house that was opened seemed to send forth something more wonderful than the last. It was difficult to choose under these circumstances, but finally three extraordinary rarities possessed of magic virtues were brought to them, and they decided on these without more ado.

The first was called *Kwagenkei*. It was a musical instrument, and if once the chords were struck the notes would never die away, but would ring on for ever.

The second treasure, *Shinhinseki*, was an inkstone box for the making of Indian ink. The owner of this treasure on lifting the lid found ink always rubbed ready for use, and the supply was inexhaustible.

The third treasure, *Menkofuhai*, was a beautiful crystal,

in whose clear depths was to be seen, from whichever side you looked, an image of Buddha riding on a white elephant. The jewel was of transcendent glory, and shone like a star, and whoever gazed into its liquid depths and saw the blessed vision of Buddha, had peace of heart for evermore.

Kohaku's rapture knew no bounds when these priceless treasures were laid before her, for she knew how happy the old priest of her own temple, far away in Japan, would be when he saw them, and with what exalted pleasure and pride, and with what burning of incense, he would place them in the temple. In an ecstasy of gratitude she knelt at her husband's feet thanking him in a thousand pretty speeches for the gifts.

Then they both sent for the Admiral Banko, and gave the *Kwangenkei* the *Shinhinseki*, and the *Menkofuhai* to him, commanding him to take his best ship and to sail with them speedily to Japan, and then to deliver them safely to the chief priest at the Temple of Kofukuji.

"Hold these three marvels of China dearer than your own life, Banko," said the Empress, " and quickly bring me word from the high priest there. Especially do I charge you with the Sacred Crystal of Buddha—guard it with your life."

And the Admiral took the precious gifts, and vowed that with his life he would answer for their safety.

We must now take leave of Kohaku, leaving her a

happy wife and queen, and follow Banko and the Sacred Crystal across the Chinese Sea.

III.

THE Admiral put the treasures on board one of his largest ships with great care, and having chosen the most experienced sailors he could find in the whole of China, he set sail. Fair winds and weather favoured him till he was within sight of the shores of Japan, when, just as he was congratulating himself and his men on their good luck, and even as he was sailing into the bay of Shido-no-ura, of the province of Sanuki, a fierce tempest arose.

Admiral Banko feared exceedingly lest he should lose his ship with all hands and her valuable freight. In that anxious hour he turned his whole attention to the navigation of the vessel, for the coast he was approaching was wholly unknown to him and his sailors, and great was the storm and their danger. Never had they encountered such a sea before. The waves rolled mountains high, the thunder roared, and the ship was tossed to and fro like a shuttlecock. There was one moment when the ship rolled over to such an extent that it seemed impossible that she should ever right herself, and all gave themselves up for lost.

Then suddenly, when the storm was at its worst, and Banko had made up his mind to a watery grave, there came a lull in the tempest. The weather cleared, and the Admiral on looking round found to his relief and joy that they were in the harbour itself and near to land. On realising his safety his first thought was to go and look at the treasures, wondering if they had been harmed in any way during the storm and consequent rolling of the ship. On going below he found the *Kwangenkei* and the *Shinhinseki* quite safe, but, to his utter dismay, the most sacred and most valuable of all the three, *Menkofuhai*, or the Buddha-reflecting Crystal, had entirely disappeared. He stood transfixed with horror, and a cold sweat broke out on his forehead when he saw that the remarkable jewel was gone from its place.

" How and where has it gone ? " was the question that he asked himself over and over again. Being a ball, it might have rolled out during the tossing of the ship, and was either in some corner near at hand or at the bottom of the sea. Or had someone stolen it ? But that was impossible, and he put away the thought as preposterous. Calling all his men, he hunted in every nook and cranny of the ship, but it was nowhere to be found.

Then the Admiral's face grew white as death, and he felt for his short sword wherewith to kill himself, for it was certain that the Sacred Crystal was lost, and he remembered how the Empress had especially charged him with the responsibility of the safety of the jewel and its delivery at the Temple of Kofukuji. He was disgraced indeed ; but no—this was not the time to take his life.

He must first do all that lay in his power to find the lost treasure ; if that failed, his knife must do its work. There was only one thing to be done now ; that was to land, and then to hasten to inform Kamatari Ko, the father of the Empress, of the disappearance of the crystal.

This he did with all speed. No words can express the consternation of Kamatari as he listened to his daughter's envoy, but he was quick to guess the cause of the loss of Buddha's Crystal.

The Dragon King of the Sea had stolen it ! This was the solution of the mystery. Riu O, the Sea King, had heard of the wonderful crystal being sent to Japan, and had coveted it for himself. Master of the sea, it had been an easy matter for him to raise up a storm so as to distract everyone's attention from the treasures on board, to the imminent danger of the ship and of their own lives.

This he had done, and when the storm was at its height he had slipped on board and stolen the crystal. Having obtained possession of the jewel, he had stilled the sea and sent the ship quietly into harbour. The agency of the Sea King accounted for the suddenness of the storm and of the calm afterwards.

Kamatari Ko did not tell the Admiral of his suspicions, but promised to do his utmost to find the jewel, which was probably lying somewhere at the bottom of the sea, and to set about having the waters searched where the loss had occurred, for well he knew the vagaries of the King of the Sea, and that, doubtless, as soon as he had got the much-coveted crystal, he had thrown it down and left it on the floor of his kingdom, the sea.

So, ordering some of his vassals to attend him he went down from Nara to the port of Shidono-ura, in the provinc of Sanuki, with the determination to recover from the sea the Buddha-reflecting Crystal. At last he arrived on the beach, and the smiling, treacherous, wonderful sea was before him, burnt and kissed to liquid jewels by the morning sun.

There also he saw, riding at anchor on the now smooth bosom of the waters, the big ship that his daughter had fitted out and sent laden with valuable treasures for her fatherland. He smiled with pride and satisfaction to think how his ambition for her had been satisfied. She was indeed the wife of a king now. But to work—he must find the crystal.

Numbers of sun-bronzed fishermen were on the beach, just as you may see them nowadays hauling in their nets, or pulling up their boats and mending them. Kamatari, followed by his attendants, went up to one group, and told them that a crystal had been lost in those very waters, and that to anyone who would go into the sea and bring it to him he would give a large reward—large enough to make the finder rich for the rest of his life.

One and all, the fishermen voluteered to do his errand. Eagerly they threw down their nets and ropes and dived into the waters to hunt for the lost treasure. They were full of hope and confidence that they would find the stone, if it were there, for they knew themselves to be as much at home in those waters as the very fish which they caught in their nets daily. But in a little while they all came up to the surface panting and blowing and shaking the water from their bodies, and made their way to the great man who was waiting for them. They held out their empty hands, and told him that they had searched the bottom of the sea in vain—nowhere could the crystal be seen.

Kamatari was disappointed. He sat down on the shore with folded arms, while his servant, kneeling, held up a big umbrella, or canopy, over his head. The ripples rolled in at his feet over the shining sand, seeming in their ebbing, flowing dalliance to mock him, as he sat there thinking what he should now do to find the lost jewel. All around him his men were silent and abstracted, for they saw how worried their chief was.

Suddenly, as he sat here, his thoughts worlds away, he was aware of a poor woman kneeling before him. How long she had been there Kamatari did not know, for he had been lost in thought. He looked at her wonderingly seeking to know what she wanted. He saw that she was a very poor *ama*, one who earns her livelihood by picking up the shell-fish on the beach. In her arms she carried a tiny infant; and, when she saw that she was noticed, spoke :

" Great Lord, pardon me that I presume to address

you, but it may be that I can help you to find what you so anxiously seek. For I have lived on this shore all my life, and know every inch of it above and below. I beseech you, bid me seek for the crystal at the bottom of the sea."

Kamatari looked again at the woman before him; he saw that she was thin and ill, and that she carried a nursing child, and he thought it a strange thing—her request.

"Do you," he asked, "a weak woman with an infant in your arms, think that you can do what all those strong fishermen have failed to do?"

"Yes," answered the woman. "I am a poor weak woman, as you see; but nevertheless, if you will listen to me I will dive to the bottom of the sea, and will bring you back most surely the lost jewel; but in return I have something to ask of you. May I speak?"

Kamatari decided to listen to the petition of the shell-gatherer, and, nodding his assent, said:

"What is it you want of me?"

"It is not for myself," answered the woman, "it is for the child I carry in my arms that I ask a favour. I am its mother, and though I am so poor and of such low estate, it is the one wish, the one prayer of my life, that my little son may be a *samurai* one day; that he may be properly educated, and that he may have a chance of being something better than a poor fisherman. Alas! I cannot teach him to read or write, and unless you help me, he must live

and die a poor fisherman as his father and grandfather
have done before him. I beseech you take the child, and
when he is old enough train him in your service as a
samurai, so that he may escape the utter poverty of his
birth. This is all I ask ; surely it is a small boon from a
great man like you. If you grant it, I will fetch the jewel
from the sea, even though I lose my life in doing so."

"That is an easy matter," said the great man,
consenting to the wretched mother's petition. "If you
get me the crystal, I will most assuredly bring up your
child as a knight, and satisfy your mother's ambition,
which I fully understand, and with which I sympathize."

And as he spoke he remembered his own ambition for
his daughter, and the recollection made him lenient.

"Will you indeed take my child and bring him up
even as your son ? Will you give me your word as a
samurai ?" asked the woman, as if unable to believe what
he said and wishing to make sure of his promise.

"I will indeed, my good woman. If you fulfil your
part of the contract, I will fulfil mine, as surely as my
name is Kamatari, the Grand Vizier of Japan."

A smile illumined the poor shell-gatherer's face for an
instant. She bowed and withdrew to a little distance to
prepare herself for the task. Giving the child to one of
the fishermen standing near, she slipped off her upper
garments, then tied a long rope round her waist, and into
this rough belt stuck a short sharp knife, wherewith to

defend herself against any monster ot the deep who might attack her. By this time several fishermen had gathered round her, lost in amazement at the daring of the woman. Many tried to deter her, telling her that they had hunted in vain for the crystal, and that she was only undertaking a fool's errand in going, and that she might possibly be drowned, and what then would become of her fatherless child ?

To them all she answered not a word, but walking out to the rocks she took up the end of the long rope and gave it into the hands of Kamatari, who with his attendants had followed her.

"When I find the crystal, honourable Lord, I will pull the rope, and your attendants must haul me up as soon as they can."

She then plunged from the rocks into the sea and was gone. Kamatari, his attendants, and the fishermen stood speechlessly watching the place where the woman had dived into the sea. They all feared for her. It was a thousand chances to one that she whould never come up again—she might be seized with cramp, or be seriously hurt among the great rocks, or be eaten by some sea-monster. So the fishermen spoke among themselves.

But Kamatari heard them not. He sat silent, looking over the rocks into the ever-whispering but uncommunicative sea, holding the rope in his hand, wondering if the poor woman would ever come back with the crystal, and wishing that he could make the wild waters tame enough to answer his questions and to tell him the secret of Buddha's Jewel, tame enough to roll the treasure up from its depths and in at his feet ; but tney were wild and heeded him not, and he sat there waiting, waiting, waiting.

IV.

Meanwhile the woman dived deeper and deeper into the sea, until at last she touched the bottom. She marvelled at her own strength, for she seemed to be unconscious of any exertion. As far as she could see all around her stretched rocks and seaweed and sand in the wild waters. On and on she went, as if drawn by some power outside herself, never thinking of the danger to which she was exposed, for her heart was aflame with the desire to find the crystal and to earn the promised blessing for her little son. And something told her that her heart's desire would be granted her.

At last, rising up through the watery world she saw the roofs of an extensive palace before her. Then the brave woman knew that she had come to the palace of the Dragon King of the Sea, of which she had so often heard. As she stood and looked at the coral roofs and portals of the great fantastic building, the thought came to her that this was the end of her her journey, and that the sacred crystal was hidden there somewhere. She swam nearer and nearer the palace.

As she scanned it with devouring curiosity from end to end and from top to bottom, she saw that a large pagoda of white coral rose in the centre. Her eye travelled from tier to tier of the rising tower till it rested on the pinnacle which crowned the highest roof of all, and on that very pinnacle, gathering to itself all the lights of the watery world and flashing them forth like vivified moonrays, lay a shining ball. Her heart leaped into her throat, for in that glistening point of light she recognised the lost treasure—Buddha's Crystal.

She could scarcely believe her eyes, and looked and looked again. So intense was her excitement and so eagerly did she gaze at the crystal on its lofty perch that she did not notice that the palace was surrounded by ferocious-looking dragons. They were the guardians of the Sea King's Palace, but so seldom was the place disturbed by anyone that they all lay blinking and dozing in blissful and unsuspecting security. But the woman knew, directly she saw them, that small indeed would be her chance of getting possession of the jewel or of carrying it off, were the monsters to catch sight of her. She stopped to think what she should do. The fear of pursuit from those horrible dragons made her tremble, but to turn back now was impossible. She could not return to Kamatari empty-handed. She had come thus far through the sea to the gates of the Sea King's Palace, and was now within very sight of the lost crystal ; she must get it or die in the attempt. And if she could reach that crystal and take it—oh, happy thought !—her child would be saved from hopeless abject poverty, and she would win for him the noble career of a *samurai*. With this inspiring knowledge she laid her hand on the knife in her belt and drew it ready for use.

Then up she sprang through the sea to the top of the white coral tower, where the crystal lay. Up, up, up ! what an eternity it seemed before she laid her hand on the shimmering jewel and caught it to her bosom ! Would those dragons with gleaming scales only sleep on till she was well away and safe with the jewel beyond their reach ? No ; the very moment that she snatched the crystal from the tower they seemed to awake from their sleep and to see her; they opened their fiery eyes, raised their great front claws, and with lashing tails rushed through the water after the thief.

She poor woman, felt that all was lost ; but with the courage of desperation she turned to defend herself, flashing her drawn knife upon her fierce pursuers. But the sea-dragons were not afraid of a knife, and they came after her fast through the water. A little more and they would be upon her, and their great talon-like claws would tear the hardly found crystal from her hands. No, she vowed that they should never do that, and with a fierce movement of the knife she gashed her left breast, and forcing the jewel into the bleeding wound, hid it there, clasping her hand over the torn flesh.

Though the *ama* knew it not, these sea-dragons had a horror of anything like death or blood, for the Sea King's realm is a fairy world, nothing can ever die or be hurt there, all is perpetual life and peace, and when they saw that the woman was wounded and bleeding they stopped in their headlong rush after her and turned back.

She saw that she need fear them no more, and remembering the rope, pulled at it with all her might.

V.

THE watchers waiting on the rocks above were roused to sudden action by the rope being pulled violently, so violently, indeed, that it was nearly jerked out of Kamatari's hand. They had almost given up hope of ever seeing her again, but now they set to work to haul the poor woman up. As length after length of the rope came up they noticed that the water was tinged with blood, and thinking this very strange, they all pulled the faster. At last the poor shell-gatherer appeared, lost to all consciousness and bleeding profusely from the big wound in her breast. She lay on the beach like one dead, and Kamatari's heart sank, for although in one hand she clutched the knife, the other was empty and was caught to her breast, and he came to the conclusion that she had not been able to find the crystal, or having found it once had let it go, when she had fainted in the depths. But what was that great bleeding gash in her breast ?

" Brave woman," he thought, " she has done her best to do my errand, and even if she has lost the jewel, I will do for her son what she besought me to do."

Restoratives had in the meantime been brought, and the woman slowly came back to life. She opened her eyes, and taking the crystal from its hiding-place she placed it in the astonished Kamatari's hand and said :

" I have fulfilled my word—do you not forget what you promised to do for my son."

" Brave woman," said the great man, and his eyes grew deep and dark with emotion, " fear not. Your son shall be as my son and shall enter my service as a *samurai*. On Buddha's Crystal, which you have restored to me, I swear this."

And as he spoke he raised the crystal with both hands to his forehead in an act of reverence. But the strength of the woman had gone. She was unable to speak her thanks. A fleeting smile of contentment passed over her face, and showed that she understood and was grateful and satisfied. She sank back to the sand and the rocks with a groan and died.

Kamatari Ko, the great state minister of Japan, stood looking down at the poor shell-gatherer's corpse. He was much moved, and it was some minutes before he spoke. Then he said to his attendants :

" This day have we seen a worthy example of self-sacrifice and of faithfulness to purpose. The woman that lies dead before us gave her life for the sake of her child. We cannot tell what happened to her down in the sea, but

"TAKING THE CRYSTAL FROM HER BREAST, SHE PLACED IT IN THE ASTONISHED KAMATARI'S HAND"

it is evident that rather than run the risk of losing the crystal, she cut herself regardless of the pain and buried the jewel in the wound, thus voluntarily made. All this she did so that she might win a hopeful future for her son. We may all learn much to-day. This woman had the true spirit of the *samurai*, and her son shall surely be one."

He then ordered the body to be taken up reverently, and he gave money for it to be buried in one of the great temples on the hills overlooking the sea.

Kamatari now returned to Nara carrying with joy the Buddha-reflecting Crystal, which, with the other two treasures, he and the Chinese Admiral took to the Temple of Kofukuji and delivered to the high priest there in his daughter's name. The Admiral Banko then returned to China to tell Kohaku that he had fulfilled his mission and to relate all that had befallen the Sacred Crystal.

And Kamatari took the motherless infant to his home and reared it as his own child. In due time, when the boy grew to manhood, the great man made him a *samurai*, and adopted him as his son even as he had promised the boy's mother, the finder of Buddha's Crystal.

At last the young man succeeded Kamatari in office as a state minister, and on learning the sad story of how his mother had sacrificed her life to buy him the heritage of a *samurai*, to her noble memory he raised a temple in the harbour of Shido-no-ura. This temple is known as Shidoji and is visited by pilgrims to this day.

" THEN HE PADDLED HIMSELF UP THE RIVER IN HIS TINY LAQUER BOWL "

Issunboshi

MANY, many years ago there lived in the province of Setsu and the town of Naniwa, now called Osaka, an old man and an old woman. They were a sad and disappointed old couple, for the great wish of their lives was to have a son to carry on their name and to pray for their souls when they were dead, and this was never granted them. They said to themselves that even if they had a child as small as one of their little fingers they would be fain content, but the years had passed by and had not brought them even this meagre wish born of a vanishing hope.

At last they determined to ask the gods for help. They shut up their cottage, the old woman putting everything in order in the house, and the old man giving his last sweep to the tiny garden. Not a speck of dust was to be seen on the mats, nor a stray leaf on the irregular-stoned, pathway, as the old couple turned for a last look at their little home, first at the porch and then at the bamboo gate, before they pattered " katta, katta" on their " geta" (clogs) down the road, and were lost to their neighbour's sight.

Thus they departed on their pilgrimage to the shrine of the deified Empress Jingo Kogo, at Sumiyoshi. Having reached the place, they made their way at once to the temple, and, kneeling before the altar, prayed her to send them a child, even though it should be no bigger than one of their fingers.

With all their souls they lifted up their hearts and their clasped hands, praying for that which had been denied them so long, and the deified Empress had compassion on them in their sorrow and pitiable old age. As they prostrated themselves in silence, quite spent after the fervency of their supplication, they heard a voice from behind the bamboo curtain say :

" Since you wish so earnestly for a child, your prayer shall be granted. I will send you one to gladden your old age."

Then the old man and woman rejoiced greatly, and it seemed as if they would go on bowing and murmuring speeches of gratitude for ever before the altar. At last, however, they rose from their knees and turned their steps homeward.

" What a joyful home-coming it was ! Even the crows' " Ka, ka " in the morning, and the frogs' croaking chorus at night seemed a new song in their ears. The old woman put red beans in the rice she cooked for the first meal, and the old man went out and bought five sens' worth of sake to make merry over the promise they had wrested from fate.

Ten moons passed, and then sure and enough a little babe was born to the old woman. Strange to say the infant was no bigger than the wee, wee dolls that are put to represent people in the miniature toy-gardens that ornament the corner of a Japanese writing table.

The old couple threw up their hands in astonishment, and for some minutes could only gaze at the morsel ot humanity before them. Then they remembered their prayer, and how they had said that they would be content if the child they longed for so ardently were no bigger than a finger.

"What fools we were," they said to each other. " Surely it would have been as easy for Jingo Kogo to give us an ordinary-sized infant as this little stick, but ' shikata ga nai'" (there is no help for it), and they smilingly made up their minds to endure what they could not alter.

They called the tiny fellow " Issunboshi" (one inch priest), and, in spite of his ridiculous size, they reared him with much care and love, hoping all the time that one day he would shoot up into a son of whom they could be proud.

But alas ! Issunboshi never grew larger, and when he reached his thirteenth year he was as small as when he first saw day—just the size of his parent's little finger. The disappointment was so great to the poor old couple, who had centred all the hope and love of a lifetime on this child of their old age, that it now outbalanced every other feeling. They began to hate the sight of the child, and one day the old man said, grumblingly :

" Though in deep humility and the desolation of childlessness we begged for a child, no bigger than a finger, yet we had no wish to be the parents of a deformity, as this son really is ! "

And they both thought that the deified Empress had served them very badly.

But it was the mockery of the neighbours which finally made them lose all patience, for when the child went beyond the bamboo fence of his home, the people would cry :

" Look ! a grain of corn is taking a walk abroad! " and when they heard him cry they would laugh aloud and say.

" Why, there is Little Finger crying ! " and so on.

Thus the unfortunate parents could not send him out to play because of the neighbours' laughter, and they could not bear to see him at home because he reminded them of their misfortune. So they consulted each other as to what they should do, and they decided to rid themslves of their strange child.

Calling Issunboshi to them the father spoke :

" Issunboshi, how is it that though we have taken the utmost care of you till to-day, you never grow at all, but remain just as ridiculously small as when you were born ? You are our son so we cannot say that we cease to love you, but we are ashamed of keeping you always in our house. Your mother and I both feel the disgrace of being obliged to own such a dwarf for our son. So please Issunboshi, my son, you must go off somewhere, and take care of yourself from to day. Go anywhere you like, only don't trouble us any more."

The little fellow, who was as good as he was small, took his parent's unkind dismissal quietly, and with all submission.

" All right, father," he said, " if you tell me to go, I will certainly obey you and leave home this very day, but, as a parting present, please give me a needle, one of the needles that may mother uses in sewing."

" Whatever do you want a needle for ?" asked his mother.

" I shall use it as a sword," said Issunboshi.

"Ah," exclaimed his mother, "a needle will be just the right size for you," and she got him one.

Issunboshi then took a piece of straw and sheathing his sword with it, stuck it into his belt.

"Okkasan" (mother), said the tiny fellow, "I want to ask for one thing more. Will you please give me a small soup-bowl and a chop-stick?"

"And what will you do with a soup-bowl and a chop-stick?" asked his mother.

"The bowl I shall use as a boat, and the chop-stick will serve me as an oar," answered Issunboshi.

"They will be just the things for you," said his mother, getting them.

Issunboshi seemed quite happy having got the soup-bowl and the chop-stick, and bidding his father and mother good-bye he went forth into the world.

He made his way to the river with his bowl, and getting into it, paddled away, with his chop-stick as an oar. In this way he left the town of Naniwa behind him.

"Where shall I go?" was now the question which occupied his thoughts. Then the capital of Kyoto flashed into his little mind as a place that would be worth while going to see. He had often heard his father and mother talk of the wonderful town, of its great temples and theatres, of the Palace, and the houses of the great Court nobles. Surely there was much that was beautiful and grand to be seen in the chief city of the land.

But how was he to find the way?

" I must ask someone first," said Little Finger, very wisely.

So he called out to the next boatman that passed by, and was told that if he kept on up the river he would soon come to Kyoto, the capital of the West.

Then he paddled himself up the river in his tiny lacquer bowl, just as you see him in the picture. It was hard work, indeed, for Issunboshi, for he and his boat were very small, and the river was wide and deep, and its current so strong that sometimes he was all but washed away.

But, as is often the case with small people, his heart and will were larger than his mite of a body. Like the pine-tree which keeps its greenness even in the depth of winter, in the midst of difficulties he never lost courage, but day after day patiently worked at his chop-stick oar. It took him a long, long time. Sometimes he stopped under a bridge to sleep, another time he stayed his bowl in the shadow of the bank of the river or a large stone, and in one month from the time he started he arrived at Kyoto.

In those days Kyoto was the capital of Japan. There lived the Emperor, surrounded by his Court, just as he lives in Tokio now. Little Finger was lost in astonishment, for he had never seen anything like this great town in the whole of his lifetime. The streets were gay and crowded, the houses large and fine, and it seemed to

Issunboshi as if all the people were dressed in holiday attire, so beautiful were the robes they wore, for he did not know that Kyoto was the Paris of Japan. He walked on and on, forgetting everything in the novelty of all he saw. How different was this city, with its clean, regular streets, its parks and temples, and its gay people, to the little town of Naniwa, his birthplace. He told himself that he was glad he had come.

Wandering along, he came at last before a large, roofed gate. Issunboshi did not know it, but he had come to the residence of one of the greatest " Kuge " or Court ' nobles, that of Prince Sanjo. With the simplicity and fearlessness of ignorance, attracted by the magnificence of the place, he, who ought to have been afraid of setting his foot inside the gate, marched right into the grounds and up to the large porch, and called out :

" O tanomi moshimasu " (I beg to make an honourable enquiry).

At that moment it chanced that the " Kuge" himself was just inside the entrance.

"What a queer voice !" said the great man, and he looked out. But as he was not expecting anything so small as Issunboshi, he could at first see no one. Thinking this very strange, as he had certainly heard someone speak, he looked and looked again, and, at last, on the step before the entrance, by the side of a pair of clogs, he saw what looked like a tiny doll, alive.

" ON THE STEPS HE SAW WHAT LOOKED LIKE A TINY DOLL ALIVE."

Oh, oh ! said the Kuge, " look here, what a strange
thing I have found ! Come, servants, come and look ! "

Then he spoke to the midget.

" Did you call just now ? "

Issunboshi bowed and said :

" Yes, it was I ! "

" Indeed? And what may you want ? " asked the
Kuge Sanjo, and, he continued, "what a tiny mite you are !
I never in my life saw anything so small as you. Tell me
who you are ? "

" I have just come from the town of Naniwa, and my name is ' Issunboshi.'"

" What ! Issunboshi is your name ! It must be because of your size that you are so called. What has brought you here ? "

" I have been turned away from home by my father because of my size, and, as I have nowhere to go, please take me into your house. Can you do so ? "

The Kuge Sanjo reflected a moment and then answered :

" Truly I am sorry for you, poor little man. You are certainly of interest to all who see you, for surely there is not such another boy as small as you in the whole world. Yes, I will let you stay."

And in this way Issunboshi entered the noble house of the Kuge Sanjo. In spite of his absurd size, Issunboshi was withal a clever little fellow, and always had his wits about him. He never forgot anything that he was once told, and never did a careless thing. Everyone in the great household grew to love him, and someone was always calling for " Issunboshi ! " " Issunboshi " and his quaint little sayings and doings endeared him to the hearts of all.

But more than anyone else the young Princess Sanjo liked the midget, and she made him her page. Wherever she went Issunboshi followed her.

Soon after his instalment into the princely family, the

Princess had to make a visit to the Temple of Kwannon, the Goddess of Mercy. She often went to this shrine to pray for the aversion of all sickness and evil from her family, and to place her own life under the protection of the Heavenly Mother, under whose feet are the dragons of the elements and the lotuses of Purity. It was not far,

"SHE SET FORTH, ATTENDED ONLY BY HER TINY PAGE, 'ISSUNBOSHI.'"

and, the way lay mostly through her father's estates, so she set forth, attended only by her tiny page, Issunboshi.

They both reached the temple without any mishap, and the Princess said her prayers, while the priest rang the bells and chanted litanies. All was soon finished, and the lady and her page had got half-way down the long flight of wide stone steps which led to the temple, when two great " oni " (goblins), hiding in the shadow, rushed out at them.

The Princess was very frightened, as well she might be, at the ugly apparitions, and ran as fast as she could, but one of the " oni " outstripped her, and was about to lay hold of her, when Issunboshi came up with him. He whipped out his needle sword from his belt, drew it out of its straw sheath in a second, and flourished it in front of the goblin, crying with all his strength :

" You blind and ignorant fool ! Do you not know who that lady is that you dare to lay a hand on her ? I am Issunboshi, in the service of the illustrious Kuge Sanjo, and the noble lady whom I humbly follow is his honourable daughter. Let go, you ignoramus of the manner of princes ! if you dare to lay a finger on the Princess, I will make holes through your rude body with my sword."

The goblin laughed aloud at the little fellow before him, and the sound of his laughter was like the banging of a brass bowl.

" You bean-seed of a mortal ! I will swallow you

whole before the Princess, as the cormorants swallow the trout in the river, if you brag like that ! "

And, without more ado, the goblin seized Issunboshi, clapped him into his mouth and swallowed him whole, just as he had said. Now, as the " oni " was very large, Issunboshi, tiny as he was, was not put to any inconvenience, as might have been supposed. Still clutching his sword, he slipped down, down, down till he found himself in the monster's stomach. Then he set to work to bore his way out, working his needle sword round and round.

" Aita ! Aita ! " cried out the goblin, in his agony. He gave a great cough, and Issunboshi was tossed into the world again as quickly as he had been swallowed up.

But the second goblin, seeing his companion wounded and groaning in pain, was furious with Issunboshi, and. screamed out :

" You are not going to escape me ! " and with these words he caught hold of Issunboshi, and tried to swallow him. But Issunboshi preferred the light of day to the dark depths of a goblin's inside, and determined *not* to slip down this time. He managed to climb up into the monster's nose. He then walked out through what seemed to him a long tunnel, but which was in reality the " oni's " nostril, on to his cheek, and then, with a mighty effort, plunged his sword into first one and then the other of his enemy's eyes.

Smarting with pain, and quite blind, the goblin felt sure

that Issunboshi was a wizard or some evil spirit, for no ordinary mortal of his size could do what he had done. He and his brother goblin had better run away before they were killed outright, and. yelling to the other monster to follow him, he took to his heels and ran for his life.

Both goblins were soon in full flight.

" What cowards you great things are ! " cried Issunboshi after them ; " you run away from *me*, oya ! oya ! oya ! " and he laughed aloud.

The young Princess meanwhile had hidden herself in a corner, trembling with fear, while her favourite midget fought her battles for her. Issunboshi watched the goblins out of sight, and then went up to her and told her there was nothing more to fear.

" Do you think you can walk home now ? " he said. " It is getting late, and we must not waste more time."

"What joy to be safe again!" said the Princess. " You have saved my life, Issunboshi, for surely those ugly monsters would soon have killed me. When we get back, I shall tell my father of all you have done, and I know that he will handsomely reward you."

Presently, as they went along, they came across a wooden mallet lying in the road before them. The Princess was the first to see it.

" Look ! " she said, " there is a small mallet lying in the road. The goblins must have dropped it in their flight. What a treasure we have found ! " and she picked it up.

Issunboshi thought it strange that his lady should show so much joy over finding such a seemingly valueless thing as this piece of shaped wood, which she had just taken out of the dirt, and he said :

"Princess, may I ask you a question ? What is the thing called that you have just picked up ? "

The Princess laughed sweetly.

"O, Issunboshi, you have still something to learn, if you don't know what this is," and she held the mallet up. "It is indeed a valuable possession. Whoever has it is quite rich. You have only to wish for anything you may want, and knock this mallet on the ground, and whatever it may be that you wish for, drops out. Have you never heard of the magic mallet ? "

"Princess," said Issunboshi, eagerly, "is it really true that this mallet has the power of giving one whatever one may wish for ? "

"Yes, it is quite true. My grandmother used to tell me when I was a little girl all about the wooden mallet' and how very lucky it was to find it. Whoever has the mallet can have at once anything they wish for. Now is your chance, Issunboshi; if there is anything you wish for, tell me and I will knock it out for you."

Issunboshi walked along, deep in thought. His eyes were fixed on the ground. All of a sudden he lifted his small head, and the princess saw that his face was lighted up as with some sudden hope.

" Princess," he said, slowly, I have a great wish! I want to be as big as other people."

" Why, of course," said the kind Princess. " I ought to have thought of that. It must be very inconvenient for you to have so small a body in this world, especially when it comes to doing things and fighting ' oni.' The magic mallet shall give you what you long for—height and size."

Then, lifting up the mallet, she knocked it on the ground, with these words :

" O height! come out so that Issunboshi may be as tall as ordinary mortals. Come out, come out, O height !"

And as the Princess knocked the mallet she looked at Issunboshi, and as she looked he seemed to grow visibly, shooting up till he was as large as a full-grown man. Astonishment made her silent, but Issunboshi felt the change, and cried aloud in his joy :

" What thankfulness ! what thankfulness, to be at last like other men. From this day forth I shall no longer be called ' Little Finger' or Issunboshi.' "

His delight was a pleasure to see. Issunboshi, quite forgetting that he was out walking in attendance on a great lady, began to dance in his exultation, pacing here and there in a slow measure with one hand on his sword and the other holding his fan on high. The Princess did not reprove him, for she knew that this was a momentous crisis in his life, and in a second he recollected himself, and bowed an apology.

It seemed to the lady and her page that they reached home very quickly after that, for the way, however long, seems to have no length when one is happy, and the Princess was as happy as her protégé rejoicing in the good fortune that had befallen him.

She related to all in the big house how Issunboshi had saved her life and dispersed the evil goblins. Then she presented Issunboshi, no longer Issunboshi, to her family, and told them of the magic treasure they had found on the way home, and how, through its means, Issunboshi's transformation had taken place.

The astonishment of everyone was great. Issunboshi was congratulated on all sides with bated breath. The Kuge Sanjo ordered him a splendid outfit to be made from the best silks and crapes, and when next he went to court, he told the Emperor the strange story.

"I am curious to see this Issunboshi," said the Emperor, and he summoned the transformed lad to his august presence.

In those days the Emperor was considered a sacred being—the Son of Heaven is his name to this day—and the greatest honour and happiness that could befall a loyal Japanese subject was to set eyes on him. This was the summit of earthly ambition, and this great joy came unexpectedly to our little hero.

The Emperor was so pleased with Issunboshi that he commanded him to be presented with many gifts as a mark of royal favour, and then he bestowed on him the rank of a high official.

Thus, after many troubles and difficulties, did our little Issunboshi win through to bright days of prosperity. In time he rose to be a great lord, with his retinue of vassals, honoured and respected throughout the land, and when his kind friend the Princess was married by her family to a neighbouring Prince, the most beautiful and the most costly wedding presents she received were those sent by Issunboshi.

And the Kuge Sanjo, when Issunboshi was old enough to take a wife, gave him his youngest daughter in marriage, and they lived happily ever afterward.

The Kettle of Good Fortune

MANY, many years ago, in the place called Tate-bayashi, in the Province of Kodzuke of Japan, there stood a Buddhist Temple called Morinji. Like many another temple, it stood in the shade of lofty pine trees, where the big, black crows held parliament the first thing in the morning and the last thing at night.

The chief priest of the temple was an old man. Every day found him solemnly serving in the temple and burning the incense before the great Buddha, dressed in his flowing robes and big rosary of crystal beads. Many pupils had he under him ; young bonzes whom he trained in the faith of the Lord Buddha, whose duty it was to walk after him, lifting his long vestments, and to move his chair from place to place while he recited the prayers before the different altars.

When his duties in the temple were finished, the O Sho Sama, or Mr. Master Priest, spent the greater part of his time in studying and performing the elaborate formalities of the ancient tea-ceremony, known as Cha-no-yu. This was his only amusement.

Whenever he went for a little walk, he pottered round to the curio shops, hunting for rare and antique vessels for his hobby, and he soon became known as the " Cha-no-yu Priest." Well, one day, as he stood before one of these old shops wondering whether it was worth while to stop, the owner came out and, bowing to the ground, said " Master Priest, I have something to show you to-day if you can spare a minnte of your honourable precious time"; and going to the back of the shop, the man brought out a strange-looking kettle and set it down before the priest.

As soon as the old priest set eyes on the kettle,*

---

*A Cha-no-yu kettle is of a different shape to an ordinary kettle.

he knew that he had come upon a treasure for his pet ceremony. It was very, very old and, therefore, valuable, and besides that, its shape was in perfect taste.

" I shall never find another kettle like this," he said to himself; and, overjoyed at his fortune, he bought it and carried it home to the temple, and put it away in the cabinet with the other utensils used in the tea-ceremony.

For a few days he was very busy, and had not time to think of his new acquisition. Then came a quiet afternoon ; he was too tired to care for a stroll, and he sat down upon the mats with a weary sigh. Suddenly he smiled, and the winter was driven from his face by the sunshine of that smile, for he had remembered the kettle. So he went to the cabinet, took out the kettle, and setting it on its box, he looked at it with ever-increasing satisfaction.

Then from the drawer of his writing table he took out a crape duster and a hawk's feather and sat rubbing and dusting his kettle with great care and pride till he began to grow sleepy, and his shaven head went bobbing and nodding " kokkuri, kokkuri," over the low table, and at last he was fast asleep.

Now a wonderful thing came to pass. The kettle, which had stood on the box before the old man till now, suddenly began to move of its own accord. It seemed to give a shake all over ; then it put forth a furry head, then four feet, and last of all a bushy tail, jumped down from the top of the box and began to walk round the room.

The priest slept on, all unconscious of the strange transformation, while the walking teakettle pattered round the room, and whacked, as if in anger, its long tail against the screens and mats.

Some young bonzes were sitting studying in the next room, and hearing strange unaccountable noises in their master's apartment, peeped in from the " fusuma " (sliding paper screens which divide one room from another). Some of them leapt backwards with astonishment at the sight which met their gaze.

They saw a tea-kettle walking about on the legs of a badger, with a head in front and a tail behind. Then they all cried out " Taihen da ! Taihen da ! " " Oh, look, look ! how dreadful! The tea-kettle is bewitched ! What shall we do ? "

Hearing their excited talk, another bonze ran to join them. " We must be either dreaming or out of our senses," said the new-comer, "to see what we are seeing. There is the tea-kettle walking about on feet ! "

" Look, look! It is most uncanny ! The creature is coming this way," exclaimed one. " Take care, I don't like the look of the thing ! "

Then all the young priests entered their master's room and called him.

"HOW DREADFUL ! THE KETTLE IS BEWITCHED !"

" Master Priest, Master Priest, wake up, please; something strange has happened."

The old priest opened his eyes, saying drowsily, " What is the matter ? How noisy you all are ! "

" This is not the time to ask questions," said the boldest of his pupils. " Look there ! feet have grown out of the kettle, and it is walking about the room now, look ! " and the speaker pointed to the other side of the room.

" What do you say ? " said the bewildered old man. " Feet have grown from the kettle ! Where ? Where ? "

Then the old man rubbed his eyes and looked about him for the walking tea-kettle, when, lo and behold ! there it was quietly sitting in its old place on the box before him, in its usual form. So he would not believe what the young priests had told him.

" What foolish boys you are," he said to the bewildered young men. " Isn't the kettle here before me ? "

The young priests looking at the kettle and hardly able to believe their own eyes, exclaimed in a breath : " Oya, oya, oya ! (Oh dear, oh dear, oh dear !) This is most strange ! It was certainly walking just now, but——"

" But—— " said the priest, " there is nothing to be said. Here it is as before. They say a pestle sometimes puts forth feathers, but in what country do feet come out of kettles ? You have told me a false story, and my nice

afternoon nap is spoilt. Fools that you are ! Go away !
Be off with you ! Quick ! "

Being thus scolded for their kind intentions, all the
young men were obliged to retire to their room, grumbling
as they went. They were positively sure that they had
seen the kettle walking about on the legs of a badger, and
they hoped ere long to show the old priest the miracle
and to convince him of the truth of what they had told him.

That very evening, while they were thus ruminating,
the old priest, wishing to make tea, filled his precious
kettle with water, and put it on the charcoal fire to boil.

Without warning, the kettle jumped off the " hibachi"
(brazier) and screamed : " It burns me ! It burns me ! "

The priest quite terrified, cried out : " How dreadful !
My tea-kettle is bewitched into a badger! Who will
come and help me ? "

Hearing his cry, all the neophytes rushed in at once ;
but, strange to relate, when they had caught the kettle,
its hairy feet and head and tail vanished as before, and
they held but an ordinary iron kettle. They knocked it
with their knuckles, but the only reply was " kan, kan,"
the sound of metal.

Their master apologised for having doubted their
word earlier in the day, and they left him alone once more
with his kettle, glad that their honour was vindicated so
soon.

Now the old priest sat thinking ; the uncanny incident

had greatly upset him, and when anything was on his mind he always talked aloud.

"What have I done? What sort of thing have I bought? While I was congratulating myself on the treasure I had found, such an unforeseen transformation takes place. It is evidently under some spell and will cause me no end of trouble. What shall I do with this kettle?"

He sat rubbing his bald pate, thinking very hard to try and find some way out of his dilemma. There was silence in the room, and only the charcoal in the brazier crackled suddenly and sent flying some bright sparks. At last the old priest started to his feet as a thought flashed through his mind.

"I have it! I shall sell the kettle as soon as possible, that is the best way. Such a peculiar utensil is useless to me. Yes, yes, I shall sell it and then it won't bother me more."

The next morning, a "kuzuya" (a man who goes about buying up old clothes and rubbish) came round to the temple. The priest knew the man well, and as soon as he saw him, brought out the kettle of which he wanted to rid himself.

The buyer of rubbish was an honest man, and after looking at the piece of antique iron, and never dreaming of anything unusual in what lay before him, said:

"O Sho Sama, this is a kettle in excellent condition,

and of some value, why in the world do you want to sell it ? Have you not made a mistake ? I assure you that it is a pity for you to part with it."

"Yes, that is true," said the priest. "I don't want to part with it, but the other day I bought a better-shaped kettle, and as two will be in my way, I shall sell this one."

"Oh, is that so?" said the simple kuzuya. Then I shall have the honour of buying this one if you will condescend to sell it.

He took out a purse from his girdle and put down four hundred *mon* (a mon is a little coin with a hole in the middle, and four hundred *mon* would be about forty cents in modern Japanese coin), and carried the kettle to his house in the city.

The priest rubbed his rosary thankfully that night and felt as it a mountain of anxiety had rolled off his back.

*　　*　　*　　*　　*

The kuzuya was very happy over his bargain, which was a splendid one, for he knew that he could sell the kettle for ten times what he had given for it. The more he looked at the kettle the more delighted he was.

"I have not made such a good bargain for a long time !" he said to himself. "And it was quite an honest one too. for I told the priest that he was parting with

" IT IS A PITY FOR YOU TO PART WITH IT," SAID THE KUZUYA

something uncommon.   Buddha is good to me, and I will send out for a little " sake " (rice-wine).

This he did and slept soundly and dreamed of Fuji-yama and a hawk the most fortunate of all dreams.

In the middle of the night he was roused by someone calling his name very shrilly : " Kuzuya San ! Kuzuya ! " (Mr. Kuzuya !)

He sat up quickly, in his fright catching hold of his little wooden pillow, and looked about him. To his utter amazement he found that the kettle which he had bought that morning was standing on four legs, with the head and tail of a badger.

No words can express the poor man's fright. He looked and looked at the curious sight, and the more he looked the more bewildered did he become. Then he spoke to the kettle :

" Ya ! ya ! (here, here !) Are you the kettle which I brought home a few hours ago ? "

Without the least fear or embarrassment the extraoradinary kettle came towards him, walking over the mats, " hiyoku-hiyoku" (as the Japanese express the sound of walking).

" Are you surprised, Mr. Kuzuya ? " asked the kettle-badger, or badger-kettle, with a twinkle in its eye.

" Ought I not to be surprised ? " said the astounded man. " I thought that you were a metal kettle all this time, and I awake in the middle of the night and find you walking about my room with a head, a tail, and hairy feet ! Who would not be surprised at such a sight as you ? I beg you will tell me what you are ? ”

The kettle smiled blandly and said :

“ I am called Bunbuku Chagama, the Tea Kettle of Good Fortune, and I am a transformed badger.”

“ Oh,” said the kuzuya, “ then you are not a true tea-kettle after all?”

“ No,” answered the animal, “ I am not a true kettle, but I shall be of more service to you than a real kettle ? ”

“ What do you mean ? “ asked the kuzuya, “ What do you mean ? ”

“ I am quite different to any ordinary tea-kettle,” said the queer badger, “so if the one who owns me treats me kindly and with respect, he will certainly be fortunate ; but if anyone should use me as that irreverent priest of Morinji did, he will lose all and gain nothing. Do you know how the priest served me ? He actually poured cold water into me, and then set me on the charcoal fire, and even after I had put out my beautiful tail (the badger switched the proud member from side to side), he called others to catch me and to strike my sides ! Why, how can I, a respectable badger, put up with such usage ? ”

And the badger puffed out his sides with great indignation.

“ You are most reasonable,” said the man. “ But would you be happy if you were always placed in your box and put into a cupboard ? What is your idea of comfort and happiness ? Please tell me."

"Ah!" said the badger, "you are certainly a wise man. Of course, if I am shut up in a box, I cannot breathe freely. I am a living creature, you know, and I sometimes wish to go out and to have some nice food to eat."

"Why, certainly," said the man. "I sympathise with you."

"When I was living in the temple," continued the badger, "I could hardly endure my hunger, and I sometimes crept out to look for food, but in one unlucky hour I was seen by the young priests, and scarcely escaped being beaten. They knocked my sides with their knuckles to find out what I was made of! Fancy that! Now you have behaved in a superior manner, and I cannot help thinking that there is some mysterious affinity between you and me, since I have come to you in this way. I wonder if I can trust myself to you and whether I may ask you to feed me hence-forward ? "

"Why, certainly," said his attentive friend. "Even I am a human being, and when I am trusted by anyone I never dream of drawing back. So if you will be content with what I can give you, I will see that you have enough rice every day."

"If you will be so kind, I shall be immensely grateful to you. In return I shall show you my accomplishments, and perhaps you can do something with them. I certainly do not wish to receive your bounty without doing something for it," said the educated badger.

"What do I hear? Can *you* do anything? This is hopeful and interesting. But what is your line?" asked the kuzuya.

"Anything and everything," replied the accomplished badger-kettle. "I can turn acrobat, and I can dance the tight-rope."

"That is wonderful," exclaimed the more and more astonished man. "Then I shall give up my business of rag-collector, open a show, and ask you to perform as a dancer and an acrobat!"

"That is a good plan, a very good plan," said the badger; "and if I act with all my power the whole land will turn out, and your gain will be much greater than it you remained a humble kuzuya."

"If you are as good as your word, Mr. Badger, I shall feast you royally every day."

The contract being completed thus, the kuzuya decided to open the show at once.

He lost no time, and the very next day he began to make preparations for the venture. First of all he built himself a proper hall for the performance. Then he engaged musicians skilled in playing the samisen (guitar), and the drum, and in the front of the building he hung a large picture of the performing badger.

When all was ready he dressed himself in the kami-
shimo costume (the winged dress, so called on account of
the standing shoulder pieces), a style of dress always
worn by lecturers at shows and exhibitions.

Then he took his stand in front of the building and
called to all that passed by, flourishing his fan towards the
sign-board.

"Sa, Sa" (Look! Look!) here is to be seen the
accomplished Badger Actor, the greatest discovery of
recent times. If you compare him to the dog actors or
bird acrobats you make a great mistake. This is a kettle
with the head and legs and tail of a badger. It can dance
and turn somersaults on a rope, besides other wonderful
tricks. Where in the whole wide world could you find
such an extraordinary actor, either in ancient or modern
times. Come and see the performance, and you will be
amused for ever. Turn away, and you will be great
losers. Come in, come in! Hasten, good people, hasten!
Never mind the fee till afterwards. You may pay me
when you have seen what I have to show you."

This was the speech with which the kuzuya invited
the spectators to enter. When they had come into the
hall, there was another speaker to welcome them, and
this is what he said :—

"Ladies and Gentlemen, what I am going to, show
you are the special accomplishments and antics of the
actor, Mr. Bunbuku Chagama, a genius, about to show

himself for the first time to a wondering world ! First of all he will perform a dance on the tight-rope ; afterwards he will show you various dances that you have never seen before, one after the other."

Then the speaker clapped two pieces of wood together, " chon, chon, chon." Now the actor, Bunbuku Chagama solemnly came on the stage, made a low bow to the visitors, and began his dance on the rope.

All the people were breathless with astonishment at the sight of the strange actor, and his still stranger antics. They had never seen anything like it before, and ex-clamations and ejaculations filled the air.

" How strange ! How amusing ! How marvellous ! Was ever such a curious creature seen before ? A badger with the body of a kettle dancing on the tight-rope ! Oh ! Oh ! Oh !"

And the reputation of this show spread like lightning round the city ; all the people from far and near rivalled each other in coming to see the wonder first. So great was the rush that the authorities were afraid that the house would break down, and scaffolding was built round the building to support it. In less than twenty days the kuzuya had made a fortune befitting the name of the Badger Bunbuku Chagama.

But the kuzuya was far from being a greedy man, and he began to think that it was hard on the badger to keep him working so strenuously for much longer. So one

"BUNKUKU CHAMAGA BEGAN HIS DANCE ON THE ROPE"

day, as they were sitting together drinking a cup of tea, after a good day's performance, he said to the badger-kettle :

"Listen to me, Mr. Bunbuku. It is in your honourable shadow that I have made such an exceptional fortune, and I am very grateful to you. Now I have enough to retire on, and I think that you must be tired with these endless performances. What do you think of giving up the business now and taking a rest ?"

"Yes," answered the badger-kettle, "I have no objection to make to your proposal."

"Then," said the kuzuya, "I have your consent." And he immediately closed the show, much to the disappointment of the whole neighbourhood.

The kuzuya and Mr. Bunbuku Chagama now took a week's rest together, enjoying themselves grandly and feasting on the best rice and fish that they could get for money.

Then they both went to the temple of Morinji, and the kuzuya told the priest all that had happened, adding :

"It is owing to your having sold me this wonderful and lucky kettle, that I have made such a big fortune, so I have come to thank you and to offer one half of what I have made to the temple, and the kettle will stay with you if you will treat it as such an important thing ought to be treated—with all respect, consideration and kindness."

The priest bowed his thanks and took the present of

money, all tied up in a box with red and white string, and the kuzuya departed, promising to come as often as possible to see his faithful friend, Bunbuku Chagama.

After this nothing unusual happened to the kettle, which is preserved on a gold and lacquer stand, with all honour as a valuable relic, in the temple of Morinji to this day.

The Mouse Bride

ONCE upon a time there lived in the wall of a large Japanese house a rich and prosperous gentleman and lady mouse.

They had been married for many years, and lived together as happily as fish in water. The pride of their life was their beautiful little daughter, " O Chu San," or the honorable Miss Chu, just growing up to be a lovely maiden mouse.

Her skin was white as snow, and her eyes were long in shape and of a beautiful pink colour, and when she squeaked it was like the sound of the wind saying " chu, chu, chu," and thus she was called O Chu San.

She was so clever that her parents sought out the best of masters in Mousedom for her, and she was soon versed in " Higher Learning of Mice," and the poetry and history of her country. She could read fluently and write letters in good style, a most necessary part of a Japanese lady-mouse's education.

All the other accomplishments had not been neglected

and little Miss Chu could play the *Koto* (Japanese harp), and perform the tea ceremonies and arrange flowers in exquisite taste.

In her little hole next to her parent's in the wall of the house was to be found a set of well selected books and several musical instruments, and at the time of which this story is written there could not be found a more perfect young mouse than O Chu San.

Mr. and Mrs. Mouse, of course spent a great deal more than they ought to have done in buying the best crape kimono for their daughter. Not only that, but her toilet-boxes were made of beautiful lacquer, and her metal mirror was an heirloom in itself.

The neighbour-mice, willing as they were to admit the charms of the Belle of Mousedom, laughed and squeaked a little over the absurdities of the fond parents, and said that they must be excused for going a little mad over O Chu San, for, contrary to the general rule of mouse-couples, they had had only one child. Then the sage neighbours twirled and wiped their whiskers and switched their tails from side to side, as they thought how very much wiser they were in the way they brought up *their* little mice.

But no one could deny that little Miss Chu was now in the bloom of her youth, and her father and mother, uncles, cousins and aunts held a family council as to the advisability of choosing a suitable husband for their lovely young ward.

No young man in Mousedom was good enough for their daughter ; that was the conclusion that Mr. and Mrs. Mouse arrived at, and they squeaked away all the suggestions of the interested relatives. They were not going to give their precious O Chu's hand to a vulgar young fellow of the common herd. Oh dear, no ! Only the most distinguished man in the whole world was a fitting mate for one who was so well educated, so accomplished, so great a musician, and so beautiful as their daughter O Chu.

Then the father-mouse retired to his own hole to think out what course he should take in finding a proper and suitable son-in-law.

" I wonder," he said, at last, " who is the greatest man in the world. I must find him for my daughter. Now he must be Lord Sun or Lord Moon. Lord Sun, however, is so dazzling that no one can go near him, but Lord Moon seems gentle, and his light is as soft as it is bright. I will go and ask the Lord Moon if he will become my daughter's bridegroom."

The father-mouse, whose name was Chubei, set out for the Moon, and having arrived at the softly shining orb, he made a low bow and said :

" Hail, my Lord Moon ! You are still a bachelor, are you not ? Will you not wed my daughter O Chu ? She would make you a perfect wife ! "

The Moon sent forth a dazzling ray of astonishment, he was so taken by surprise that night, and the astronomers watching the sky on earth tried to account for the great momentary brightness.

"What is it you say, O Mouse?" asked the Moon. "In all these ages you are the only one who has dared to propose that I should become his son in-law. I thank you very much for your kind offer, but I cannot accept it, for the *Cloud* separates me from all things terrestial and would be an insuperable obstacle to my union with your daughter.

The Chubei went to the Cloud and made the same proposition to him as he had done to the Lord Moon.

The Cloud stood still for a few minutes' reflection. Then he answered the visitor:

"It is true that I often hide the Moon from the Earth and am the only obstacle between his union with your daughter, but I also am fettered, and my enemy is the *Wind*. No, I regret to say that even the Cloud is not free enough to accept your proposal."

Now our poor mouse was nearly in despair, but he summoned all his courage to the fore, and hastened to the Wind, and quickly asked him if he would marry his daughter. But the Wind only blew out his huge bags and said:

"No, I am very sorry, but the *Wall* stands between your daughter and myself, for the Wall is my great adversary."

Our Mouse at last thought that he had found what he was looking for. There could be nothing stronger or

THE VISIT TO THE MOON.

more renowned than the Wall who was able to resist the
Wind, and he felt sure as he went along that the Wall
would be his son-in-law.

But when he paid his visit to the celebrated Wall,
Mouse Chubei received a long answer which effectually
damped his adventurous ardour, and his long whiskers
grew quite limp as he listened to the Wall's reply :

" Have I need to tell you, Mouse Chubei, that although
I am strong enough to resist the Wind, before your kind I
am as nothing. Where would be the wisdom of marrying
into a people who would cause my death ? Is it not the
pastime of your people to gnaw me into holes ? Your
play is my death. Great, indeed, would be my fall were I
to marry O Chu San."

" Ah," said the crestfallen mouse, " all that you say is
quite true. It is time that I returned home to think," and
so saying he bowed himself out of the presence of the
Wall, and took his way towards home.

His faithful wife, ever on the watch for his return, ran
to meet him on the threshold of their little hole-home,
eager to welcome her mousey-husband and to know the
result of his search.

As soon as the bows of meeting were over Mouse
Chubei sat down, and unwilling to give any sign of the
discouragement he had felt, pricked up his ears, and
making his whiskers stand out straight, said :

" Ah, my dear wife be proud and happy and contented

that you and I are mice ! Do you know that mice are the Masters of Creation. Listen, and I will tell you how this is true. When I set out a few days ago I felt sure that Lord Moon was the greatest fellow in the world, superior to everything, but do you know that the Cloud can master him and that his light is quite obscured when the Cloud chooses to pass before his glorious face. And again, the Cloud is not master of itself. It may be driven about from one end of the sky to the other by its foe, the Wind, which can blow it whithersover it will. And the Wind also is obliged to turn aside when confronted by the Wall. Now, perhaps, mousey-wife, you will be thinking that the Wall, being able to oppose the Wind, is lord of all. What will you say when I tell you that we mice can cause the fall of the greatest Wall ever made by gnawing it into holes. Thus it is that we mice are superior to everything ! Nothing is fit to be compared to us. Therefore, we cannot do better than marry our dear and precious daughter to some young fellow of our own kind."

The mouse-wife had listened attentively to all this long speech, and she was convinced that her husband's final decision was the right one, and she told him that she was quite of his opinion.

Now both the anxious parents of O Chu turned their thoughts to the choosing of their future son-in-law from among the circle of their near acquaintances. Every eligible young mouse that they knew was talked over as the possible or impossible bridegroom.

"What do you think of Mr. Chumaru, who lives in the roof?" said the father.

"He is a nice fellow, certainly," answered the mother, "but you forget that there is a cat living near his house. I could not bear the thought of O Chu's life being in danger of a cat."

"How stupid of me to have forgotten that. Well, there is Chukuro of the cupboard, how would he do?"

"Oh, dear no, that would never do, the dog sleeps there every night!"

What a difficult thing it was to be sure to find just the right mouse for their daughter, and how troubled they both were. There was silence for a few minutes and Mrs. Mouse rose and made some tea, and they both sipped their cups of tea hoping that some inspiration would strike them.

As they were both sitting there, looking out across the garden, very puzzled over the difficult problem, who should come up to the house on some business but their own clerk, a charming and clever young mouse. They had known him for a long time, and had often remarked what a praiseworthy fellow he was, though the thought of his marrying O Chu had never yet entered their heads.

"Look, Chubei," said Mrs. Mouse "instead of going so far away to find a son-in-law let us marry O Chu to our Clerk Chusuke. He is the very one, and there he goes ! I saw him and that made me think of him, and, indeed, where could we find a more suitable young fellow ? He is steady and hard-working, and everybody says that he will do well ; besides that his heart is in the right place, and he is handsome. He has known our child from her infancy, and they are friends and understand each others' characters pretty well. What do you think ? "

Mr. Mouse was delighted with his wife's thought. " What a splendid idea ! Chusuke is just the very fellow. He is certainly a rising young mouse and will make the best of husbands, I am sure. Why in the name of rice-cakes did we not think of him before ? "

So Chusuke, the clerk, was informed of the happy fate which his superior planned for him, and for a whole day and night he ceased not to squeak for joy at the good news. He called himself the happiest of mice, as indeed he was.

O Chu, on hearing of her parent's wish, seemed happily content with their choice, and she rejoiced that in marrying Chusuke she would not have to go far away from her parents' home, since he lived hard by, and so the matter was settled.

Now all were busy in the mouse-hole arranging the presents for her bridegroom and getting the bride ready for her new home.

A few days later a grand wedding was celebrated in

TRYING ON THE WEDDING DRESS.

Mousedom. The bride was carried in a closed palanquin to Chusuke's residence at the other side of the house, and a long procession of bearers carrying large boxes full of her possessions went before her and wound its way along the rafters of the house. The mouse-bridegroom met her on the threshold of her new home and conducted her to the room where the ceremony of drinking the three cups of wine was to take place, and there the happy young couple were united in the presence of their respective parents.

The bride's father was exceptionally merry over the marriage of his daughter, and was heard to give some worthy advice to some of his young pachelor friends.

" How I wasted my time in going to see those whom I thought great and powerful, and who, after all, were unable to accept my good offer. I found out, though, that we mice are quite equal to everything else in the world, if not better. And I learned to be coontent with what was near at hand and to know its value. It is by far the best thing to marry among your own kind. You, my dear boys, go and do likewise, and remember the proverb, ' Go farther and fare worse,' and paikoku, the God of Happiness, will bless you. And do not forget to thank him always."

The Chrysanthemum Crest

ONCE upon a time, long, long ago in Japan, there grew in a large meadow, a wild chrysanthemum bush. It was the lovely season of autumn and under blue skies of sparkling softness two little star-like flowers had blossomed among the green leaves. Sister-flowers were they, so alike that they resembled twins : they both had exactly the same shape and the same number of dainty petals in their corollas ; the only difference between them was their colour, for one was white and the other was yellow, so they were named by the other flowers of the field, who were very proud of them, the Lady White, and the Lady Yellow.

They were happy little flowers ; all day long the sun shone on them and they opened their petals wider and wider to his warm rays, and when night came they drank together of the same refreshing dew. Soon they were in full bloom, and no more perfect little chrysanthemum could be found anywhere.

One day an old man came to the field and found the yellow and white chrysanthemum blossoms in their sunny corner. He looked at them carefully for some minutes and then he spoke to the yellow flower :

"You are very pretty! Won't you come to my garden?" he said. "I am a chrysanthemum gardener," he went on smiling, "and if you come with me, I will help you to grow into a much larger and more beautiful flower than ever you can be if you stay here."

"Shall I really grow up as you say, if I come with you?" asked Lady Yellow wondering. "Is it true what you tell me? I can hardly believe it!"

"Oh, yes, it is quite true," answered the old man. I I will give you good food to eat and beautiful clothes to wear, such as you have never even dreamed of in this wild field, and you will then become a larger and lovelier flower!"

As the old man coaxed her, promising all these nice things, the yellow chrysanthemum, quite forgetting her sister, wished to go with the old gardener, for she was vain and ambitious, and longed for an opportunity to show herself in the great world beyond, of which she had sometimes heard even in that quiet spot.

"Oh," she exclaimed breathlessly, "I should so much like to go with you!"

"Will you come? Yes? Then I will take you with me at once!" said the old man delighted. He then began to dig up the yellow chrysanthemum by the roots, and having done this, turned back to go home.

All this time the white chrysanthemum had been listening to everything that was said. When she heard him ask her sister to go with him she felt very anxious, but being of a timid and retiring nature she said nothing. When however she saw that he was going to take her sister-flower forever she could bear it no longer. With the aid of the friendly wind, passing by just then, she put out one of her branches and touched his dress, saying :

"Oh, Oh! do not leave me behind! If you take my sister please take me also O Jii San!"*

"Oh no, I can't do that!" the old man answered crossly, for he was in a hurry to get home with his newly found treasure, and did not like being hindered.

"But O Jii San, don't you know that we are sisters, and that we have grown up side by side ever since we can remember? If you take her away I shall be left quite alone! Oh, please, take me too!" pleaded the white chrysanthemum with tears running down her snowy petals.

"No, no," said the gardener, "you are only a white chrysanthemum. I know by experience that you will not repay my trouble half as well as your sister. You had better stay and play with the grasses and wild flowers here! You are of no use to me!" and with these words he went away.

The nursery garden to which the old man slowly wended his way was near by, and the yellow chrysanthemum soon found herself in her new home. The O Jii San

---

* Honourable Mr. Grandfather, a term by which old men are popularly addressed.

kept his word and treated her with the greatest care and kindness.

He set her down opposite the verandah of his tiny cottage, and while he rested after his walk and took two or three whiffs from his small bamboo-stemmed pipe, his wife came out with a cup of tea for him, and he bade her admire his new acquisition.

"What a lovely flower!" she exclaimed. "Where did you find it? Oh! What a pretty flower!" Then she slipped her bare feet into her clogs and pattered up to the plant to get a nearer view, her brown face wrinkled all over like a withered apple lit up with smiles.

Then the old man set to work. He brought some water in a wooden pail and washed the leaves and petals of the yellow chrysanthemum very carefully, picking off as he did so every leaf he thought unnecessary, and every bud on the stem, so that all the nourishment from the roots should go to the crowning blossom. When this was done he dressed her in beautiful crêpe robes and gave her food to eat; and then he placed her in a sunny flower bed, sheltered from the rain and the wind by a roof made of reeds.

In a few days so changed was the yellow chrysanthemum that she hardly knew herself. Day by day under the clever gardener's care she grew to be a large fine flower, till at last her petals became so long and full and her head so heavy that she had to be propped up by a

" DAY BY DAY UNDER THE CLEVER GARDENER'S CARE SHE GREW TO BE A FINE
FLOWER."

stick. In this stately flower no one would now have
recognized the little wild flower of the field. She was very
happy and content for her dreams of reaching the fine
world beyond her native field had been realized, yet in the
midst of her new happiness and grandeur, she could not
help thinking sometimes of the sister-flower she had so
willingly left behind in the lonely meadow, and when she
remembered her sister's tears at parting and her last
entreaties not to be left behind, she felt guilty in the
enjoyment of her pleasant, easy life. At such times she

would try to distract her thoughts by looking at the gay flowers near her and by watching the visitors as they came and went round the garden. She would soothe her conscience by saying that their different lives were allotted by fate, but in her heart, she knew that, tempted by the glamour of the old man's promises she had done a heartless thing, and that nothing could excuse her conduct, yet she could not make up her mind to go back to the old hard life, which was the only path of repentance left to her. And so time went by.

One day there was great excitement in the garden and the old man ran out to the gate, for the chief of the village and two or three of his friends were seen approaching. The old woman smoothed her hair hastily with a tiny comb which, pushed just under her queue of hair, was always kept on the top of her head, and then slipping on a silken haori,* got tea ready and brought it out to the verandah with cushions for the distinguished guests.

" Look here, old man," said the village chief as he sauntered up the path between the flower beds looking to the right and to the left at the bright array of chrysanthemums, " I want to know if you have some *true* chrysanthemums ? "

" Welcome, my lord ! " replied the wondering old man bowing down to the ground and drawing in his breath as a token of respect, " but what do you mean by a true

---

* A kind of jacket worn over the kimono and the obi.

chrysanthemum ? I have cultivated chrysanthemums for many years from the wild plants, but I have never made a *false* chrysanthemum yet ! "

" Is that so? Well, I will tell you what I mean," said the chief of the village. The Lord of this Province wants to find a perfect chrysanthemum to use as a design for his crest. But the so called fine chrysanthemums are all too fantastic for his taste—some of them have too many petals, others again have petals too long or too irregular or too curling. My Lord wants a simple natural white chrysanthemum of sixteen petals, and this we cannot find so far, though we have searched diligently, asking every gardener we came across, but none of them had what we wanted, nor could they tell us where to find it. Hearing at last that you were the best chrysanthemum gardener in this province I came to you. Have you by any chance such a flower as I have described ? "

" No, my Lord, I have not, but I pray you to come this way, and I will show you a really beautiful flower," and with great pride he led his visitors to where the yellow chrysanthemum was blooming in all her glory.

" Look at this flower ! " went on the old man, a finer blossom you will find nowhere, no, not in the whole world, I am sure; will not this suit you ? "

But greatly to the disappointment of the old gardener, the chief of the village only shook his head and said:

" Oh no, I want a *true* chrysanthemum ; that is a very

fine flower, but it is too unnatural for my purpose!
Thank you for your trouble, but I must look elsewhere ! ''
and he left the place.

As the village chief was returning homewards he
happened to cross a wide field. Passing by a clump of
chrysanthemum bushes his attention was arrested by the
sound of weeping. He stopped at once and looking about
him he saw a white chrysanthemum blossom crying.

" Oh, poor chrysanthemum," he said kindly, " What
is the matter with you ? "

" My name is White Chrysanthemum. Some time ago
an old gardener came and carried away my sister the
yellow chrysanthemum. I begged him to take me with
her, but he refused, saying that he had no use for white
flowers like myself, and now I am left quite alone, and
that is why I cannot help weeping all day and all night
too. Oh, oh, I cannot bear the loneliness ! I wish only
to die and to leave this sad world ! I pray the sun to
scorch me, the wind to break my stem and the rain to
pour heavily enough to crush me to the earth, but they
never heed me and I am obliged to drag on a weary
existence. Oh, why did my sister go away and leave
me here ? Why doesn't she come back remembering the
love of our budhood ? " and she burst into tears again
and her pretty head drooped lower and lower till it was
almost hidden by the green leaves.

The kind man looked at the flower carefully and he

saw that she was as round as the full moon with sixteen perfect petals all growing simply and naturally : indeed she was the very flower he had been looking for so long ; and the tears dropping from her wistful face looked like jewels of dew, and reminded him of the poet's beautiful simile, which likens the cherry flower in the rain to a beautiful woman in grief. Ten times more charming did the white chrysanthemum appear to him in her modesty and unconscious loveliness than any of the proud and much trimmed flowers of the many gardens he had visited of late.

"This must be the very flower for which my lord has sought in vain for years," he said to himself. Then going up to the white chrysanthemum he said :

"Don't cry ! You are a beautiful flower and need never feel ashamed. What the old gardener said is all nonsense. Every one has not the same taste, I am thankful to say. Even if he cares only for yellow chrysanthemums you are very precious to me. I have seen your sister and I do not consider her half as beautiful as you. Now, weep no more, little lady ! Come with me, and you shall lead a life of usefulness and honour and great happiness too ! You have been reserved for something better than to bloom in a common garden !"

As he went on talking the white flower had lifted her head and hardly able to believe the good man's words she asked him eagerly :

" Oh, can I really be of use to you ? Is it true what you tell me ? Or am I dreaming ? "

The sunshine fell upon her now and the man saw that her sweet face glowed with hope, making her more beautiful than ever.

" Of course, you can be of great use ! My lord will be delighted when he sees you, for you are just what he wants. He has been looking for a chrysanthemum like you for a long, long time. After neglect your fate has come at last, and a wonderful one it is, as you will soon learn.

" Oh, tell me what you mean ? " said the white chrysanthemum pleadingly.

" Well you will certainly never guess," said the village chief smilingly, " so I may as well tell you at once. You are to serve as my Lord's family crest ! And as a famous crest your form and beauty and memory will live forever in the heraldry of your country. Just think what an honour fate has kept in store for you. Rejoice that you were not carried away with your sister and planted in the old gardener's flower bed, like hundreds of other flowers. You will see what wonderful days there are for you in the future ! "

So the village chief carried the white chrysanthemum home with him, and his wife and servants helped her with her toilet, and dressed her in lovely robes of silk and crêpe. When all was ready and she had. been regaled with a delicious meal, she was bidden to enter a fine palanquin and carried like a lady of noble rank, to the Daimio's palace.

"SHE WAS BIDDEN TO ENTER A FINE PALANQUIN."

When the Daimio saw White Chrysanthemum he was pleased beyond all words and said that she was exactly what he wanted for his crest. Everyone in the great household, down to the innumerable retainers, praised her beauty and perfection. She was placed on a flower stand in the garden opposite the great lord's room where he could see her at sunrise, noon and sunset. Artists were sent for from all parts of the country to come and draw designs of the sixteen-petalled chrysanthemum for his family crest. Day after day the hitherto despised and neglected flower found herself surrounded by a group of admiring artists, whose one idea was to draw her as artistically as possible.

Her different aspects were studied under every mood of the day and of nature, on bright or cloudy or rainy days. They watched her in the soft light of the morning sunshine, in the dazzling brilliance of the noon, and again when the shadows of the evening fell athwart her delicate face, uplifted to the heavens above in thankful and joyful surprise at the good fortune, which had so suddenly and unexpectedly come upon her. The Daimio and his wife, the "Honourable Lady behind the Screen," would rise before the dawn to watch the first beams of the sun awaken the pretty flower from the languor of the night to the energy of the day.

The noble pair both took pleasure in bringing her fresh clear spring water to drink and in wiping off every speck of dust that fell upon her. They invited their friends to come and see her and the gracious and modest beauty of the simple blossom gave joy to everyone.

At last the design of the sixteen-petalled chrysthemum for the family crest was finished, and the Daimio ordered it to be painted and inlaid on all his precious belongings, and the shape of the flower was fashioned in gold on all his beautiful lacquer treasures, on his armour, and embroidered on silken quilts and cushions which take the place of chairs in a Japanese house ; it was dyed upon the rich silk, and woven at the household looms on the crêpe destined for the ceremonial robes of the Daimio and his family, and in the whole of Japan to this day there is no more artistic and beautiful crest than that of the sixteen-petalled chrysanthemum.

The crest being finished the Daimio more and more pleased with the beauty of the design, for Japanese taste invariably chooses the simple in preference to the ornate, gave the word that it was to be used in the ornamentation of his house ; so the form of the favourite flower was outlined and silhouetted in black and in gold and in silver on the paper and friezes of the rooms ; she was carved in the handsome woodwork of panels and portals ; on screens she was painted floating down the undulations of a stream or wafted by the wind across a cloud ; and in pictures for the alcoves of the best rooms she was depicted growing wild as she was found, or trained against a bamboo fence ; in fact in every imaginable way and artistic combination that Japanese fancy could devise. " The fame of the white chrysanthemum and of the unique crest that had been fashioned from her, spread abroad till at last there was no one in the aristocratic circles of the capital who did not acknowledge that it was one of the most beautiful crests that had ever been designed in Japan.

Thus was patience and goodness and modest waiting rewarded at last as true worth always is.

And what happened to the yellow chrysanthemum ? Well, she bloomed in the gardener's flower bed for several autumns, till a severe frost one year killed her, and the old gardener very reluctantly, for she was his favourite and chosen flower, pulled her up by the roots and threw her out upon a rubbish heap. In the height of her pride and much vaunted beauty thus died the yellow chrysanthemum, and she left nothing behind her by which she could he remembered in the world, not even the memory of a single good or useful deed, while her long-time neglected sister, as the sixteen-petalled chrysanthemum crest was perpetuated and will hold her place in the art and picturesque heraldry of Japan forever.

So life often teaches mortals as well as flowers that good things come round to those who while doing their best in their allotted sphere, quietly wait and trust.

The Fallen Comet

AT night you can see thousands of pretty stars twinkling and sparkling in the silent heavens " with crystalline delight," but in the daytime entirely disappearing from the sight of man, they hide themselves behind the clouds and sleep away the hours until the sun sets and the night comes and the earth has need of their light.

On the particular day about which I am telling you the stars had all composed themselves for their daily sleep and snugly tucked up in their quilts of nice soft fleecy cloud, were dreaming happily of the dark velvety night when they would come forth attendant on their Queen, the Moon in all her glory, when they would give light to the sleeping world and inspiration to many a poet and artist, when they would sparkle in the still waters of river, lake and ocean, lighting many a wanderer home and guiding the sailors, who set their courses by the stars, across the wide deep lonely seas.

As they lay in peaceful slumber dreaming dreams of future usefulness and beauty, they were awakened by the sound of chirping voices, and peeping from under the soft clouds, saw two or three little birds chattering together in a most excited manner. Feeling somewhat annoyed at being disturbed from their first sweet dreams, one of the stars gave an angry sparkle and said.

" How tiresome you birds are ! What are you, and why do you come here making such a noise and disturbing us in this way ?

Then the birds chirruped :

"We are larks. Can't you see that ? Being larks we twitter and warble. Because we twitter and warble we are noisy."

The answer of the birds was so cool and impudent that the star fairly lost his temper and shouted :

" You may be larks or any other kind of birds, but you have no business here. If you want to chirp and twitter in this noisy way, why can't you go down to the earth and do it ! This is the sky and belongs to us, as you ought very well to know.

But the larks were not sent away so easily, and they began to argue the point, saying :

"We don't know what other birds do, but its the usual custom for larks to warble in a hihh altitude and therefore our name is written in Chinese characters as 'sparrows of the clouds'! You grumble about our singing, but how about your own conduct, you sleepy creatures idling away your time and sleeping all day long ? If you don't like what we say and it makes your cross why don't you get up and sparkle a little and show that you are stars and can really shine as you boast

"THE VENERABLE OLD COMET AT LENGTH AROSE"

you can ? You might be bits of dull lead for all that we can see ! "

This impertinent speech so infuriated the star that he began to twinkle fiercely and emit little flashes of brilliant light, but the larks were not at all frightened at the stellar rage ; on the contrary, they retaliated by flying round, twittering more vociferously than ever and said :

" Pooh ! who's afraid of what the stars say ? How can the stars hurt us when they daren't even go out in the daytime ?

So the naughty mischievous larks went on flying round and round just as they pleased, delighted at the idea of tormenting the stars, who they knew were powerless by day, and the noise of their singing only grew louder, and the stars behind the clouds began to give up all hope of rest that day. In the meanwhile, an influential and vener-able old Comet, who was much respected among the stars, had been quietly watching all that was going on and said to himself :

" Oh ! those mischievous larks ! The sly birds come to worry us in our resting place, because it is daylight, and are bold and impudent because they think we are helpless ; I'll frighten them a little and then, we'll see whether they cannot leave us in peace for a while ! "

So saying, the venerable old fellow unable to put up with the lark's naughty behaviour any longer at length arose, and wagging his long, broom-like hair and beard, exclaimed :

" You good-for-nothing impudent larks. How dare you behave so rudely ? If you don't fly away at once I'll sweep you out of existence and so finish you once for all ! "

Then the Comet began lashing his hair and beard all round just as one does those long white-haired brushes used in the East for driving away flies ; but the larks knew that it was daytime and that therefore the old Comet could not shine enough to frighten a mouse, so they were not in the least alarmed, but only amused at his frantic and useless efforts.

" Look at the old Comet ! What a stupid old fellow he is ! ha, ha, ha, ! " and the larks laughed a long, trilling laugh, and called loudly for their friends to come and join the fun.

The number of larks who responded to the call was very great and they flew hither and thither chirping and twittering until the noise became unbearable. Exasperated beyond all endurance, the old Comet waved his long hair and beard round with all his might until his head looked like a windmill in motion, but his efforts were of no avail owing to the overpowing numbers of the enemy, and at length he grew dizzy, and instead of driving away the larks, missed his footing, fell off the cloud, and tumbled headlong to the earth with an awful crash, where he lay in a dead swoon upon the ground.

" THE COMET FELL OFF THE CLOUD AND FELL HEADLONG TO THE
EARTH "

When the stars saw what had happened to their old leader they were terrified, and there was a great commotion up above the clouds. " Alas ! alas ! " said all the stars " the venerable old Comet has fallen down. What an unfortunate end to such a brilliant life ! "

But they were unable to do anything to help their elder. All they could do was to weep behind the clouds, and their tears fell upon the earth like rain, and people wondered what had come to pass as they looked upwards, for the skies were clear.

" The larks, on the contrary, all began to laugh and sneer, saying:

" Aha, look at him ! Doesn't he look foolish down there ? Who would have thought to see the Comet lying so low ? " and chanting a song of victory in chorus they flew down to earth again.

Now it happened that in a certain country house outside the capital there lived an old farmer, a simple man, who was never so happy as when he was tidying up his garden after breakfast in the morning and looking for the first plum blossom to appear in January or the first cherry flower in April.

On this particular day as he was walking through his fields growing emerald green with the young rice, he found what looked like a small birch-broom lying right across his path and picking it up, he said to himself !

" Oh ! Oh ! I wonder who can have left this here !

Why it's quite new ! Well, as it is of no use here, I'll take it home and use it in the house. It will just do for sweeping up my garden every morning."

As he was thus talking to himself he noticed that the handle had a beautiful gloss upon it, and shone as if it had been made of gold or silver, and on the top of the handle was what looked like a large star.

" Oh, " said the old farmer," this is indeed a fine broom. The handle looks like gold and the end like silver—it cannot be an ordinary broom—it cannot. I have heard that among the treasures of the Demon's Island brought to Japan by Momotaro* there is a magic rain-coat and magic hat, and I shouldn't be surprised if this broom proved to be some kind of similar wonder for it looks mysterious. Well I will use it and see how it works."

With these words the old man took it home and began to sweep up the garden with it. He found that his new found treasure was splendid for the purpose, much better than any other broom, he had ever used. As soon as the old man became tired he sat down in the shade under a tree, and pulling out his pipe, lighted up and was sitting himself down for a nice quiet smoke, but by accident when he flung away his match, it fell upon the broom and then a wondrous thing happened. The broom, which had hither-to seemed but an ordinary one, suddenly glowed with light

---

* See in the Story of Momotaro or the Peachling in the Japanese Fairy Book, Constable & Co. London.

" THE SEEMING BROOM SPRANG RIGHT UP INTO THE HEAVENS "

and threw out a wonderful radiance like a halo and began to hiss and sparkle and crack just like a fire-cracker. The unexpected sight almost frightened the old farmer out of his wits, and he began to run away from the spot as fast as his trembling limbs could carry him.

In the meantime the seeming broom shook itself, throwing out a shower of sparks and then sprang right up into the heavens, leaving a broad trail of fiery light behind to mark its path.

For a long while the old man stood rooted to the ground with fear ; gazing up into the sky open-mouthed in utter amazement at the unexpected thing that had happened to him, but at last he was recalled to his senses by some neighbours who came running out from their little houses near by to ask what was the matter and what was the reason of his looking so frightened.

It was some time before the old man could speak clearly—all he could say in answer to his neighbours anxious inquiries was " oh, oh," or " who would have thought of such a thing ? " and like exclamations of astonishment. At last one of the neighbours took the old man gently by the hand, for he was still shaking from the shock he had received, and led him home. Once inside his little room he sat down on the mats and lighted his pipe once more. His old wife brought in tea and a few sips of his daily beverage seemed to restore the old man. He now looked round on the assembled neighbours and bowed to them apologising for his rudeness.

Now the old farmer began his marvellous story pausing often to wipe his brow and sip his tea and smoke his little pipe. He told how walking in the fields he had found what looked like a shining broom—how he had carried it home with him and of how he had swept the garden with it—how suddenly it had caught fire, sparkling and crackling and then had shot up to the heavens like a rocket trailing a cloud of glory behind it till it had utterly vanished into the blue and could no more be seen.

You may imagine how astonished the neighbours were on hearing the strange story and the air was full of exclamations of surprise from all his friends when the old man finished and for many a long day the wonderful story was a constant theme of conversation in the village and near provinces. Visitors from far and near came to see the farmer, curious to know the truth of the tale and anxious to take back some new incident to tell their less lucky neighbours who had not the time or the means to go to see the old man.

The explanation of the phenomenon is a very simple one. The strange broom was indeed the Comet who fell in anger from the skies when trying to drive away the larks ; a comet is by- nature of a fiery composition and the flame of the match tossed heedlessly away by the old farmer when he lighted his pipe acted as a tonic on the

Comet and revivified the poor fellow. Was it not fortunate that the old man was walking in the fields just at that moment, and should have then wanted to smoke and that he happened to throw away a lighted match, for otherwise the Comet would not have been able to get home until the evening. How happy the little twinkling stars were to see their venerable elder back. safe again and they never laughed so much as when he related how the farmer had mistaken him for a broom. They were still twinkling and dimpling with laughter at the fun of the idea, when the sun set and the darkness called them forth to shine, and give light to the earth once more, and so happy were they that they never shone with greater brilliance than on that night.

The Demon Tile

L ONG, long ago in old Japan on the outskirts of a large village there stood a magnificent Buddhist temple with long sloping roofs and large courtyards where the gnarled and knotted branches of the weird old pine trees threw heavy shadows on the grey and peaceful gravestones and the stone flags of the pathway leading from the huge gate to the big still porch.

The temple looked like many another temple to the ordinary passer by, but the people of the district told a different story, for high up on the gabled roof lived a large Demon Tile. This Tile could transform himself whenever he willed into a frightful monster with horns on each side of its forehead and gleaming eyes which rolled from side to side and glinted like cold metal mirrors in the sunlight. In his angry moods he used to frown down on the villagers with a grin so terribly wicked that the little boys and girls who passed the sacred fane on their way to school were glad to hurry by the building to escape from his dreadful presence and malicious glare.

One fine winter's day when there was no wind blowing, the Demon Tile began to gaze around him from his commanding position on the temple roof and forthwith began to talk to himself.

" Oh, what a fine day it is ! " he said. The air is so clear that I can see for miles around and distinguish every object in the neighbouring town. I wonder what that big pillar is over there from which the smoke is curling up. Oh, I see now ! It's a chimney ! Quite a new thing in these parts, brought by the foreigners from over the seas, I suppose. Now what can that be over there in the opposite direction ? It looks like a ladder standing on end and has a small hanging bell attached to it. Oh, I know ! It must be a fire-bell, which if a fire happened to break out, would begin to make a dinning clang to warn the people and to call them to the rescue. If we did have a fire it would be a magnificent sight from here and I should like to see the spectacle, but I don't want it to come too near, for the temple would be in danger and especially the roof with its tiles and myself amongst them."

Thus the Demon Tile talked to himself about many things he saw, and then craning his neck farther up he glanced over the whole stretch of country before him, but owing to his exalted position on the temple roof, every thing on which his eyes rested appeared far beneath him, and small and insignificant in comparison to himself. Then he began to feel elated at his position and in his arrogant folly and pride began to think that he was superior to everything and everybody around him and he consequent-ly said to himself :

" I CAN SEE FOR MILES AROUND " SAID THE DEMON TILE.

" Who can be compared to me in all this wide world ? In my place here, am I not the most exalted of all things and beings on earth ? There is nothing higher than I am ; between me and the sky nothing intervenes, and for me to climb up to the heavens is an easy task. Indeed, I feel that I am a most remarkable person."

While he was thus pondering over his rank and dignity and making these ridiculous and conceited remarks something struck his face, inflicting a stinging sensation, and at the same time the tip of his nose grew cold and icy. This was caused by the biting north wind suddenly springing up and driving grit and sand in the Demon Tile's direction, making him blink his eyes in an attempt to remove the dust with which they had been filled. Then the Demon Tile complained loudly about the coldness of the wind and its rudeness in attacking such a sacred edifice as a temple of Buddha, and its stupidity in not distinguishing between the common tiles of the roof and himself, the chief tile of the temple. But the wind-god was quite indifferent to the Demon Tile's grumbling and growling, and calmly opened the mouth of his wind-bag still wider, letting out furious blasts of piercingly cold winter wind, which blustered and roared in the face of the Demon Tile until the latter grew wild with rage and shouted out in a terrible voice like thunder :

" Look here, you wind-god ! Why do you want to come out here at all, upsetting everybody and spoiling this fine weather ? Don't you see that you are making everything cold and miserable ? If you want to blow, go out to the mountains and the wide ocean but keep away from the town ! "

Then the Wind-god blew out his huge wind bags and shrieked and whistled round the temple and shouted angrily in the Demon Tile's ear ;

" Well, the fine weather cannot last forever, and you cannot expect the wind to be always lazy. I have my work to do in the world and must do it whether it pleases you or not. At any rate, it's my business and not yours as to whether I blow or not. If you are cold why don't you get down under the verandah instead of sitting up there on the roof. You have chosen the most exposed place you could find. I am sure it's your own fault if you are cold."

This rough unceremonious answer, exasperated the Demon Tile beyond endurance and he retorted :

" What do you mean by insulting me, you rude ignorant fellow. Do you take me for a low foundation stone ? Did anyone ever hear of a respectable tile and especially a Demon Tile living under a verandah ? "

" Suit yourself, and do any thing you like—only I warn you that I am going to blow my bags harder than ever ! "

With these words the Wind-god maliciously opened his bag to its widest extent, and the poor Demon Tile became

"THE WIND GOD OPENED HIS BAG TO ITS WIDEST EXTENT."

so cold that he shivered all over and felt that he would be frozen to death. At the same time his enemy being the Wind-god, the Demon Tile was powerless to do any thing but frown angrily and maintain a sullen silence. He now realized that he had made a mistake to anger his foe.

For some time the wind continued to blow a perfect hurricane, but after a while he seemed to get tired and gradually drew off in another direction. This pleased the Demon Tile very much, but when at length he thought himself safe he raised his head and gazed around, he noticed suspicious looking clouds floating about in the sky. These clouds had been gathered together and driven on by the wind, and gradually, as they formed together, the sky grew dark, threatening to spoil the beautiful day, and making everything gloomy and sad.

" Oh, how tiresome," said the Demon Tile, " now the wind has ceased, those banks of clouds have formed shutting out the sunshine and I shall be drenched through and through as soon as the rain begins to fall."

Hardly had he ceased to speak when soft white flakes began to flutter down, and he muttered ;

O dear! O dear ! Now it's started to snow. This is most provoking—What shall I do now ? "

Then he drew in his head and kept himself still in silent misery. He was in despair for there he was perched high on the topmost gable of the roof, exposed to the full fury of the elements, and curl himself up as he might, he could not avoid being snowed up.

The snow fell fast and thickly, fine powder-like snow which lies thicker and thicker, layer on layer as it falls, and gradually the whole of the Demon Tile's head was covered with white flakes.

Now, when the wind ceases to blow, its disagreeable effects stop at once, but when snow has collected on any thing, there it stays and freezes the object. The poor Demon Tile therefore caught a fearful cold in the head, his teeth chattered, his horns shook and he began to shiver all over. At last he felt so miserable that he could endure the torment to longer. Then he thought out a plan as he said to himself: "Am I not a Demon Tile ? There is nothing above me but the heavens. Both the wind and the snow came from heaven in the first place, so if I only went up there I should be in the same place as those detestable creatures, and then I should not be exposed to such bad treatment. Yes, it is a splendid idea ! At last I have hit on a good plan. I think I will try how it works at once. I am so high up already that it cannot require any very great exertion to get up to heaven from here—just one good jump will do it ! "

Then the proud and stupid Demon Tile picked himself up and steadying himself for the jump, faced towards the sky and counting, "one, two, three," sprang upwards. So well did he jump that he rose high above the temple roof and thought he was well on his way sky-wards ; but he soon lost his balance, and falling headlong to the earth with a dull thud was smashed into small pieces.

Under the verandah the foundation stone of the temple had been sleeping peacefully but the noise of the Demon Tile's fall awoke him, and lazily glancing around, he exclaimed :

"What was that noise, I wonder ?" Then he saw what had happened and began to laugh right merrily and addressing the fallen Tile said,

"Well, well! so you have tumbled down from the roof, have you, Mr. Demon Tile ? I am really astonished beyond all measure that such a high and mighty personage as you should show a wish to associate with common foundation stones ! Have you really come here of your own accord or is the priest repairing the roof and you have been thrown down ? Wonders will never cease ! How nice you look down here—ha, ha ! You might have been born on the spot ! ha, ha, ha !" and the foundation stone laughed again and again.

You see that even a Demon Tile may lose his high estate if he becomes too arrogant and conceited and defies the laws of nature, so I hope my readers will take warning by this little story, and remember that " *Pride goeth before a fall.*"

複製不許

印刷所　教文館印刷所
東京市京橋區銀座四丁目一番地

發行所　ケリー、ウォルシ
横濱市山下町六十番地

印刷者　デー、エス、スペンサー
東京市京橋區銀座四丁目一番地

發行者　ケリー、ウォルシ
横濱市山下町六十番地

著者　尾崎英子

（定價金一圓七十五錢）

明治四十一年十二月十六日發行
明治四十一年十二月十二日印刷